THE GOLDEN DOLLY

When the Duke of Wellington's scout, Titus, thinks he is dying in a church in Spain, he confesses he has lived the life of a rake, and vows to reform if he lives. Overheard by an imprisoned heiress, she frequently reminds him of his vow after he rescues her and takes her back to England. Once home, he must repair his reputation. And as he searches to find out who stole Helen's fortune, he falls in love.

ANNE HOLMAN

THE GOLDEN DOLLY

Complete and Unabridged

LINFORD
Leicester

First published in Great Britain in 2006

First Linford Edition
published 2007

British Library CIP Data

Holman, Anne
   The golden dolly.—Large print ed.—
Linford romance library
   1. Love stories
   2. Large type books
   I. Title
   823.9'2 [F]

ISBN 978–1–84617–906–8

Published by
F. A. Thorpe (Publishing)
Anstey, Leicestershire

Set by Words & Graphics Ltd.
Anstey, Leicestershire
Printed and bound in Great Britain by
T. J. International Ltd., Padstow, Cornwall

This book is printed on acid-free paper

1

Under fire from the burning June sun and French sharpshooters Titus Stonely ran for his life in the mountainous Basque country in 1813.

'Damnation!' He slipped on the stony ground after turning to see through his spy glass blue-uniformed soldiers approaching in the distance. He'd not shaken the French off, they were still stuck to his tail.

He swiped the sweat from his temporarily-blinded eyes as he crawled beneath a shrub, fearful it might not hide him adequately, and was alarmed at the sudden scream of an affronted buzzard he'd disturbed from its nest.

Mind awhirl with tiredness and pain, Titus tried to assess his hopeless position. Tenderly feeling his shoulder, wet with blood where an enemy bullet had entered his flesh and made him drop his rifle a mile back. He knew he'd become an easy target — and was weakening minute by minute.

Exhausted from running in the heat for many hours, Titus, who usually enjoyed a fit body now felt petrified he might die soon from loss of blood.

He'd hoped to avoid the enemy by coming over the limestone ranges and by-passing the little villages and isolated farms towards Burgos, expecting to find the British-Portugese-Spanish army marching north, but he'd misjudged the numbers of Frenchmen in the region. The area was crawling with them, all eager to catch a British scout.

Awhile back they'd shot his horse from under him. Then, hearing a piercing whistle in the air followed by an excruciating pain in his arm, Titus knew he'd been winged. The Frenchmen, like huntsmen after their injured quarry, were now enjoying the chase.

Titus realised his good luck, like an hour-glass of sand, had finally run out. His privileged birth now counted for

2

naught. His easy passage through life had come to an end. He accepted he must prepare to meet his Maker.

If only he could have another chance. He would mend his ways, but there was little chance of that he realised. He grimaced — at least he'd enjoyed his life, his carefree, rashly-spent youth.

But there was a more urgent need for him to survive a little longer. If only he could summon enough strength to reach the British lines, which he was sure lay ahead. 'Surely some friendly soldiers can't be far away,' he wheezed through his parched lips.

Yet he was confused, unsure of his direction, wondering how many miles he might have to go before encountering members of the British-Portugese-Spanish army who were trying to oust the French from the Iberian Peninsula.

Duty gave him courage. If it was the last thing he did, he would do his damnedest to deliver his important message to Sir Arthur Wellesley, the

British Commander in Chief of the Peninsular War.

His ebbing strength and searing pain must be ignored because he knew that the success of the lengthy campaign to drive the French out of Spain depended on scouts like him providing Sir Arthur with accurate information. Men willing to risk life and limb — torture even — to bring the British vital news about the enemy positions and plans in this huge, wild country.

He'd managed to get the information Sir Arthur had asked him to get, but he had foolishly — rashly, as was his nature — run straight into a hornet's nest of enemy sharpshooters on the way back to give his report.

Indeed his message would never arrive at Sir Arthur's tent — unless he gave up trying to deliver it. So he must not give in.

Titus, in this dire position, grimaced. Things might look hopeless for him, but he told himself, he was not captured yet!

Blinking rapidly he endeavoured to ignore his fatigue and pain and concentrate on where to go next. Weakened, footsore and bleeding, he knew he must get going again immediately, because to stay still was to invite a French soldier to discover him and to stick a bayonet into him.

Jupiter! Where could he hide in this rocky terrain?

The French were bearing down fast on their injured prey. He could even hear their guttural cries, their laughter. 'After him, citizens!'

'Allons! See his blood.'

Alas, they were getting nearer. Too near!

Making a supreme effort, Titus clenched his teeth and crawled out from his cover, and half standing he tottered on, climbing upwards. Suddenly his swimming eyes blinked rapidly. He was struggling to be able to focus. Was he seeing a mirage — or was there really a building ahead?

Wiping his face with his blooded

hand, Titus peered ahead again. Yes indeed, there was a solid structure at the top of this hill, as plain and colourless as the landscape in the strong sunshine.

Hearing French cries and boots tramping the earth behind him, his instinct was to hide and no other place came to his mind but to go for cover in that building ahead. He didn't know this region of Spain, or if the inhabitants were for, or against, Napoleon and the French. But what choice did he have but to risk going there and try to conceal himself?

Perhaps there would be water there — he was desperate for a drink.

Dragging himself nearer he recognised the building was a church. A suitable place to leave this world he thought grimly. Indeed, he had almost no strength left now and was leaving a trail of blood behind him which would bring his pursuers after him in no time.

The church door was open. Falling against the door frame Titus gasped for air and clutched at the wooden door for support.

Inside the small chapel cool air greeted him. He staggered in and fell prostrate before the altar praying aloud. 'Good Lord,' he cried passionately, 'I beg of you, take me before the French capture me!'

God didn't answer — and was he surprised? His life had not been saintly. He'd not won a place in the celestial kingdom he was quite sure of that! As a young English nobleman his life had been filled with misdemeanours. He was not destined for heaven — unless he repented.

'Lord, I have sinned,' Titus cried out in agony, 'broken many commandments . . . ' Now he had to be honest and admit that in his life he'd been wayward. But his mind was confused trying to remember his many faults and to put his confession in order.

He cried out, 'My conduct has been a trial to my parents. I've been lustful. I

took Lady Sands from her husband . . . ' he gulped, 'I've gambled
recklessly . . . stolen . . . ' he gasped for
air, 'and frequently drunk myself silly.
And — '

'Oh, for heaven's sake, spare us any
more!' a soft female voice, in English,
sounded, abruptly stopping Titus's
declaration.

Appalled he'd been overheard, Titus
turned his head to find the owner of the
voice.

A lively nun was coming towards him
with springy footsteps. Embarrassed to
see she was young — and no doubt
innocent — he cringed. She'd heard his
confession! For once in his life Titus felt
heartily ashamed to think of his past
misdeeds. He'd have been a lot less
explicit about his sins if he'd known
someone was listening!

She was barefoot and had neat feet
and ankles. But Titus quickly reminded
himself that this wasn't the time to be
thinking of such things.

'I'm dying,' Titus groaned, 'done for!'

'That, I very much doubt,' the little nun replied crisply as he noted the faintest smile on her attractive features. She had a rosy apricot complexion, which reminded him forcibly of women he'd known in England. She must be English. Her accent was perfect. Her eyes were an intense blue and looking at them he felt he had dived into the ocean.

'Forgive me, sister, for invading your chapel. I will leave . . . ' He bit his lip to prevent himself from crying out as he tried to rise to his feet. 'As soon as I can.' He gave a groan. 'I've been shot,' his fingers splayed out over his wound.

'I can see that! You've left enough blood all over the floor and I'll have to wipe it up.'

Titus looked back towards the door and grinned. 'Well the floor's tiled so you won't have difficulty cleaning it up,' he retorted. 'And it's blue blood,' he added with a chuckle. Then thinking of the relief his noble parents might feel,

knowing their younger son had per-
ished and would do their name no more
harm, he hid a sob.

The nun clasped her small hands
together. 'I think I need to wipe you up
first, then I'll do the floor. Mother
Abbess will be furious if she sees this
mess. I'll get a cloth and a basin of
water. Stay where you are.'

'I wasn't thinking of going anywhere.
French soldiers are outside baying for
more of my blood.'

Hearing this, the small nun seemed
scared. Vulnerable. Her sapphire eyes
glinted before her lids lowered. Had the
nuns been informed that the fighting
had come to their region? Had the news
spread to her remote convent of the
horrors of war? The plundering and
destruction the French had done
during their time in Spain and Portugal? Did she know about the killing
— and violation of women?

Perhaps she did, that was why she
was now silent. Was she praying?

Titus looked more closely at the

sister swathed in shapeless garments and veil. She was too young — and too pretty to be a nun!

'Don't worry, sister. I'll go — when I can get on my feet again.'

'You shouldn't. You're hurt,' she said, kneeling down beside him and looking at the gaping wound without flinching as though she was a nurse used to seeing torn flesh. 'I'll have to get Sister Joan to tend your wound.'

He couldn't prevent a moan escaping his lips before he replied, 'Don't worry about me, I'll be off in a minute, sister, but I beg you to get an important message to Sir Arthur Wellesley.'

'Who is he?'

'The commander of the British forces. He should be somewhere near Burgos. It is vital you get this pouch to him.'

She looked down at the small leather dispatch pouch he was anxious to give her.

'Go on, take it. It won't bite you!'

'I don't know if I should . . .'

11

'Heavens girl! Don't you want the British to win this war?'

She seemed reluctant to take it. She hesitated and looked at his pleading eyes before her delicate hand took it. She fingered it as if it were red hot as she looked at it askance with her head on one side. Then she enquired in a hushed voice, 'But, sir, how can I possibly get this out of the convent to your commander?'

'Well, hide it then. Make sure the French don't get it.'

She obediently slid it under the folds of her serge habit.

'Now, go. Hide. The soldiers will be coming here soon and you must not let them find you.'

He groaned as he fell back. He'd done his best. With any luck the message might be delivered. Anyway he'd got rid of it. The French wouldn't find it on him before they shot him.

Titus's last prayers were mumbled, begging the Lord to protect the young nun. He lay back on the floor. He'd made his last confession. He was ready to die.

But the skeleton of death did not come and open the door for him. There was no convenient exit from life for Titus Stonely.

Instead, there was a commotion at the door as French soldiers crowded into the church with oaths and shouts of triumph. 'Vive La France! We've found our English spy!'

'Kill him!'

'No, get him outside first, then we can 'ave a little fun with him!'

Titus, in horror, began to shiver. He hoped death would come quickly.

Then a screech filled the chapel. A sharp female voice, like a banshee, sounded in Spanish. 'Get out, you rabble! This is a house of prayer. A sanctuary. Do you all want to be burned in hell for violating God's holy house?'

The French soldiers, unshaven and battle-hardened, stood open-mouthed. Some swore and others crossed themselves. They had no time for religion, but French soldiers were superstitious. Always afraid some omen of bad luck may strike them.

The Spanish female drew in breath and yelled again, 'I am the Abbess here. You soldiers get out of our chapel. Immediately!'

Titus knew he couldn't move, but then he realised the harridan was not addressing him.

The French soldiers had halted their advance towards the prone man. Their faces leered at a wall of nuns who had suddenly appeared before them. The sisters were a mere pack of unarmed females against swarthy battle-hardened French soldiery. Yet under their uniforms many of the Frenchmen were Christians, unwilling to harm God's brides.

Some were afraid of ill fortune for desecrating a church. Others, well, didn't they have wives that yelled and scolded like this shrill abbess? Best to keep away from the likes of her.

Fearful for the nun's safety, Titus

cried out, 'Take me. I'm over here.'

But the abbess continued to sound over his voice like a siren. She was a volatile Spanish female whose barrage seemed to lift the very roof off! My God, it scared Titus — let alone the nuns that woman ruled, and now she seemed to be affecting the French soldiers. Stopping their advance.

'Let's get out of here. That Englishman's going to die anyway. Can't you see his blood comrades? He's had it.'

They didn't hesitate for long. Bowing and walking backwards, the French soldiers retreated out of the church. Some crossing themselves again and again. Some offering apologies and some got stuck in the doorway in their haste to retreat.

Titus managed a tiny chuckle. He was suffering agony and was certain he was dying, but whatever else he'd lost — especially his dignity after relating all the shameful secrets of his life — he'd not lost his sense of humour.

When the soldiers had gone the nuns

crowded around him. The hard-faced abbess was staring at him too. Would she have him thrown out? He became aware of the little nun he'd first met and given his message to, looking scared, her head lowered before the abbess who was ranting at her.

Was she refusing to give her superior the pouch he'd entrusted to her? Then he fainted.

2

Titus awoke in great pain. He was lying on a pallet in a tiny room no bigger than the butler's pantry at home. One slatted window let in lined shafts of sunlight, light enough for him to observe his shirt and breeches, cleaned and pressed, on the chair by the washstand.

His head thudded. Someone had stripped, washed and shaved him, and tended his arm, which was now bandaged. And he was alive! But the throbbing pain seemed unbearable and he wished he wasn't alive to suffer it.

He struggled to think, where was he? How long had he lain there?

The convent bell sounded. Dong, dong, dong. Ah yes, he had taken refuge in a convent. And there was a young nun . . . thinking of her sweet face, Titus fell into blessed unconsciousness again.

Hours later, little Sister Lucia stood by his bed.

She was mesmerised as her eyes examined him. At the age of twenty she felt hungry for the sight and feel of a young man. And it was exciting to be able to talk to a person who spoke her language.

Such thought would be sinful for a nun. Impure. But she wasn't a proper nun. She'd been put in the convent at twelve years of age and had no opportunity to leave. Wasn't she the same as any ordinary young woman with a natural curiosity about the opposite sex? Wouldn't she choose to marry and have children — if she had the choice?

And after hearing the patient's confession, she knew that the British spy who lay before her on his sick bed wasn't pure either. My goodness what a long list of sins he had confessed!

When he batted his eyelashes and his slate grey eyes opened, it reminded her of misty mornings in England she had almost forgotten.

As his eyes contacted hers, she exclaimed, 'There now, I hope you're feeling better.'

She knew he must be in pain. And he was a sinful man, she knew all his faults, didn't she?

She unashamedly continued to feast her eyes on him. And it wasn't entirely pleasant for her, because when he moaned and winced, she felt the pain too.

The infirmary nun, Sister Joan, who'd removed the bullet from his shoulder was no surgeon, and had done the best she could. In a poor, isolated community like theirs, they had to be self sufficient, and make do with what was available.

At least Sister Joan had saved his life. She'd kept the wound clean, free of infection. So he hadn't died as the sisters thought he might.

Even the Mother Abbess had told the nuns to pray for the young man that he might continue his life serving his God

— she didn't know that the sick man was far from being the God-fearing young man she thought he was!

Sister Lucia was not supposed to be in the infirmary cell, but she'd slipped in when everyone had gone to the Angelus. She knew she would be scourged for missing the Angelus, and again, severely, if caught in his cell. And her back was still sore from a whipping she'd received recently for some other infringement of the convent rules. But her inner soul told her she was not sinning in the eyes of the Lord. And she felt certain it was her duty, as an Englishwoman, to assist this man.

She held a pitcher of water and a cup for the patient, and was anxious to tell him his message to Sir Arthur had been sent.

Still feeling dazed and in great pain, Titus lifted himself up gingerly to regard her. 'How long have I been here?'

'Sister Joan removed the bullet from your shoulder several days ago.'

'Several days ago,' he repeated in wonderment. 'So you reckon I'll live?'

She nodded and keeping half a wary eye on the door she tip-toed nearer offering him a drink, and whispered, 'I gave your message to a pilgrim going to Santiago de Compostella, who came by begging for food. He was on the way to Burgos.'

Titus gave a groan. 'That's a fat lot of good!' he gasped. 'The French are in Burgos.'

'You don't know the latest news, sir. We understand the English have marched by Burgos and are assembling at Vitoria.'

'The pilgrim's way does not go through Vitoria.'

She nodded and replied calmly, 'I know that is so. But EI Camino goes through Burgos which is not far from Vitoria.'

'Humph! I suppose there is a faint chance the missive might get to Sir Arthur.'

Annoyed her difficult task of getting the message out of the convent was not appreciated, she retorted. 'What else could I do? I'm not free to walk out of here, you know.'

With light steps she went to the window and looked out over the mountains. How she longed, every day, to escape.

Titus cleared his throat. 'I'm sorry,' he said, 'I gave you an impossible task. I'll just have to hope the information gets to my commander.'

She swung around to look at him. Her nostrils flared. 'I assure you I could do no better.'

His eyelashes flickered. She had spirit this little nun. No wonder she was disciplined by the abbess! She probably was here with him now when she should not be.

Feeling he'd been ungrateful he assured her. 'Sister, you did well to get the message away. Just say a prayer that it will arrive in Sir Arthur's hands in time.'

Suddenly he tossed and cried out. Fearful his cry might bring another nun into the cell, she came towards him saying urgently, 'When you return to England, would you deliver a message for me?'

He regarded her serious expression. 'Of course I will. If I ever get there.'

Her anxious little face came nearer his. She said in a soft, urgent voice. 'I want you to tell my aunt where I am.'

'And your aunt's name, is?'

'Lady Sands.'

Horror showed on his face. The humiliation of his loud confession in the chapel made him cringe.

'Yes, Lady Sands is my aunt, sir.' She didn't add, that is the lady you admitted you'd seduced.

His mouth felt dry. He stretched out his hand to accept the cup of water. Sipping the liquid, he said, 'I suppose you think ill of me having heard my confession in the chapel?'

'We are all sinful, sir.'

'But, you know I am worse than most men.'

She gave him a shy smile. 'So? I'm

told I'm worse than most nuns.'

He smiled briefly. Her readiness to accept that everyone was not perfect made him warm to her.

Then he grimaced with pain and she knew she should leave him to recuperate. But as she made towards the door she said. 'I don't know your character, sir, and withhold any judgment I might make of you. I only know you are my only chance of getting a message to my family.'

She gave a sad sigh and looked at the bare stone wall of the cell. 'Although my aunt may not be interested in me anymore, after all this time. She may not believe what you tell her.'

Knowing Lady Caroline Sands he breathed in deeply. 'Of course she will believe me. I'll do my best to get a message to her. What is it you wish to tell her?'

'That I am held a prisoner here.'

He gulped. 'You are truly a prisoner? Here?'

'As good as. I am barefoot as all the

nuns are. I can't walk far in this stony country. Besides I don't know the area. I have no money. I can't leave the convent.'

Titus was suffering so much pain he found it difficult to concentrate, but he could well believe it would be nigh impossible for the girl to walk on the sharp, stony earth without shoes. And this convent was miles from anywhere.

Perhaps poor youngsters who grew up barefoot could manage without shoes. He certainly couldn't.

He struggled to think above the pain, and then faded into unconsciousness.

It was hours later before Titus was able to speak to her again. Having been washed and his wound dressed, he observed Sister Lucia was fetching and carrying for Sister Joan. He quickly thought of a reason to dismiss the older nun and was able to talk to her alone.

'There will not be much time before Sister Joan returns so tell me quickly, what was your name before you entered the convent?'

She whispered back quickly. 'Helen Martindale.'

His mind buzzed. He'd heard of that name. Yes, indeed. 'Helen Martindale? The missing heiress?'

Helen breathed a sigh of relief. He had heard of her. She was amused to be known as the missing heiress when she lived in poverty. She replied hurriedly in a hushed voice. 'I was brought here when I was twelve, soon after my parents died. I was grieving and easily tricked into believing I was going on an exciting expedition abroad, not expecting to be incarcerated in a convent for the rest of my life. So I came willingly.'

Observing his rapt attention to her story she continued, 'I wish I was back in England. I don't want to be a nun.'

'But it is criminal to keep you here against your will!'

Helen nodded. 'But who cares I was young and spoilt, and had just lost my parents, so I was easy to coax into coming here. I didn't realise I'd never get away.'

She'd been a little fool. She had been too trusting, and was now paying the price. She didn't think Lady Sands knew what had happened to her, neither did her grandmamma, her governess, and the house servants, who would have missed her.

Titus was enthralled to be hearing about the missing young heiress. Her fortune was known to be massive, that was why Society talked endlessly about her. She had been presumed abducted, kidnapped, or put in an asylum, but there was no proof that she had been. The young lady had just vanished, disappeared.

In fact, she had the reputation of being a bit wayward — like himself. So the *ton* accepted she had been a victim of misfortune after years of her not being found. That was why her estate had been taken over by her uncle.

Titus stared into her entrancing blue eyes. She had admitted she was, like him, far from being perfect. Was she telling him the truth? Was she just a young, fanciful nun who had made up a story to enliven what must be a hard, dull life for her here in this remote convent? Or had he really stumbled upon the rich girl there was such a mystery about in England? And he knew more about her than most, as he knew her aunt, Lady Sands . . .

Helen would have explained more only there was someone hurriedly treading down the corridor and the cell door suddenly crashed open.

The two nuns that rushed in grasped Sister Lucia and bundled her out of the door with a torrent of Spanish.

He caught a glimpse of her face distraught. Her eyes beseeching him, before they were lowered in passive resignation of her captivity, and she was quickly bundled away.

Titus lay back and thought alternately of his pain, and the extraordinary story he'd just heard. Maybe, if he got the chance, he could test Sister Lucia and find out if she was who she said she was. Ask her questions that she should know the answer to. After all he knew about her family, didn't he? He should be able to find out for certain whether she was the missing heiress.

And if she was, wasn't it the gallant thing to do to help her escape this convent life she seemed unsuited for and told him she didn't want?

He'd promised God that if he had a second chance in life he'd change his ways, and that is what he intended to do. When, and if, he got back to England he would be a different man. He would be a more patient and considerate man. And would endeavour to make his long-suffering parents proud of him.

And, if he could, he would begin by trying to assist unhappy Sister Lucia. He promised himself that he would deliver her message to Caroline, Lady Sands. But before he left the convent he would find out as much as possible about the incarcerated young nun.

Sister Joan came in later to dress his wound — without Sister Lucia. Titus, who spoke Spanish well, asked her, 'Is Sister Lucia English?'

'Si, senor.'

'How did she come to be here, in this Spanish convent?'

'Senor, you will have to ask our Mother Abbess.'

Titus flinched as the wound was cleaned with a stinging ointment. And the thought of having to confront that awesome senior nun made him squirm again. He decided he would enquire further about Sister Lucia — when he felt stronger.

And seeing nothing more of Sister Lucia in the days that followed, and as his health improved and he was permitted to walk around the cloisters daily for exercise, he finally decided he should not put off seeing the fierce abbess any longer, and requested a meeting.

3

Titus removed the shift he'd been wearing during his illness and washed himself. He found it difficult, but he managed, telling himself that he would have to be patient and cope with one hand until his arm had fully mended. Then he shaved as best he could with no mirror. Convents, he was told, didn't have mirrors.

He put on his clean drawers, breeches, and his shirt the nuns had mended where the bullet hole had been. His boots were the very devil to put on without the help of a valet. He was sweating by the time he'd finished.

Hair combed, and fully dressed, he straightened his lithe body, as if he were about to go on a military parade. Taking a few deep breaths he left the infirmary cell preparing himself mentally to meet the Mother Abbess. Much as he detested parades, he thought he would have preferred to be going on parade than confronting that powerful Spanish nun.

Marching through the cloisters he considered the possibility of leaping over the convent wall and escaping the coming meeting. But now that he'd become a reformed man, he couldn't bring himself to be so ungrateful. This community of nuns had saved his life. He had to thank the abbess. He wished he had some way of repaying them. He bowed to a couple of nuns he walked past in the passageway and they smiled and nodded to him.

Obviously some of the women were happy being at the convent. Which brought to his mind one who was not.

The Mother Abbess's door was no more imposing then the rest of the poor convent building. But it was ajar so Titus put his eyes to the crack and peered in. Mother Abbess was sitting behind a table, crouched in her chair like a perched hen.

'Enter!' the abbess shrilled, making him jump.

His nerves had been shot to pieces like his upper arm. Titus straightened himself, wondering if he should knock, when the voice inside squawked again, 'Come in, come in.'

Titus swung the door open and stood shaking. He told himself that was because he hadn't fully recovered. But in truth the nun scared him.

'Do sit down before you fall,' the Mother Abbess commanded and indicated an upright backed wooden chair as she glared at him.

Titus was glad to sit. The abbess was quite right, he might have fallen. They regarded each other in silence. He frowned, not knowing the etiquette of convent life. Was he supposed to talk first?

'Umm. Ma'am.'

'Reverend Mother,' she corrected him.

'Ah yes. Reverend Mother. I regret to say I'm not a Catholic.'

33

'Being British, I didn't expect you were. Although I summoned a priest the first night you were here, in case you died.'

Titus was reminded of why he'd come. Long ago in his childhood his parents had tried to drum into him some good manners and saying thank you was one of them.

He didn't think for a moment that a priest could have saved him from his just punishment, but he appreciated her kind thought. His head swam but his military training enabled him to hide his feelings. 'Reverend Mother,' he said politely, 'I have come to thank you, and your sisters, for saving my life.'

The abbess nodded. 'It was God's will.'

'I'm sure it was — although your nuns undoubtedly helped. My arm is on the way to recovery.'

Her heavy jowls wobbled as her eyes looked steadily at him. 'So now you are off to fight more battles, I suppose?'

Titus felt he was fighting one right

now. 'I'm an army captain, Reverend Mother, and have my duties to perform.' Then he added, 'Just as you have yours.'

She actually smiled a little.

Encouraged, he proceeded, 'I'll repay you for your hospitality. Unfortunately, my money has gone.' He didn't like to admit he hadn't any prospect of acquiring any in the future either. Reckless gambling had cleaned him out. His father, the Earl of Parkham, had long since given up bailing his younger son out of debt.

The abbess got up and opened a drawer in a heavily-built cabinet. She brought out his pouch and emptied it so that the coins it contained clattered on the table.

The blood drained from his face. He didn't mind that the wily woman had already got his money, what crossed his mind was that his message in the pouch had not got through to Sir Arthur. Sister Lucia may have thought she had handed it to the pilgrim, but the abbess may have stopped it from leaving the convent.

Titus felt his anger rise. But he had to control it, realising he was now a reformed man, but he couldn't change into being mild tempered overnight. He gulped. 'You are welcome to keep my money. But that pouch also contained information that should have been sent to Sir Arthur Wellesley,' he blurted out.

She looked at him calmly. 'You mean to Viscount Wellington. We've heard he has been promoted after his victory at Salamanca. Your message was sent to him.'

What could he do except smile back at her?

He could have left at that point. He'd thanked her, and she had the little there was of his money. He had done his duty — but not quite.

Sister Lucia's wistful face came to mind. What he was about to step into was like a trap, he warned himself. But he had become an honourable man now, hadn't he? Damsels in distress were females knights of honour were supposed to save. And wasn't Sister Lucia such a damsel?

'Hum. About that English nun . . . '

'Sister Lucia?'

He shuffled in his chair, looked out of the window, but the deep blue sky was all he could see and it was no help. Perhaps, honesty — another virtue he should practice — would help. 'Sister Lucia told me she wants to leave the convent.'

'Ah yes. So she does. But where am I to send her? Life is hard here. We take vows of Poverty, Chastity and Obedience. But, I'm sure you know, Captain, that life can be even worse outside these convent walls for an unprotected young woman.'

He'd seen some miserable poverty in his travels. Some young women looking far older, and more worn, than they should be. 'Yes, indeed,' he agreed nodding.

They looked at each other with more understanding. Titus sensed the abbess might not be as awful as he had first thought. He cleared his throat. 'Well, I understand Sister Lucia has an aunt in England. I happen to know Lady Sands.' He couldn't help himself from blushing.

'Oh, indeed?'

'Well, that is, if she's telling the truth about her name being Helen Martindale, and Lady Sands being her aunt.'

The abbess pressed her lips together and leant over the desk towards him. 'I am well aware of Sister Lucia's many faults, sir, but she is not to my knowledge dishonest.'

Titus blinked. The abbess did seem to be remarkably well informed — for a nun. So he could probably take her word for it that Sister Lucia was Helen Martindale.

She went on, 'I believe she was dumped with us as a young girl by some unscrupulous relative who wanted to be rid of her.'

Now they had come to a perfect understanding, because that was what

Titus had understood too. 'Yes,' he nodded his head, 'someone did the dirty — I apologise for my language — I mean they've hoodwinked her out of her fortune.'

'Fortune?' The abbess's voice was raised as if she were calling someone.

'Helen Martindale had a great fortune, ma'am, I mean Mother — '

'That would explain it!'

'Explain what?'

'Why she has been abandoned here!' The Mother Abbess leant back in her chair and folded her hands under her ample sleeves. 'I suspected some evil at the back of it. Someone contrived to send the child abroad so that they could benefit by her absence. We accepted the child, thinking we were looking after her temporarily. But after eight years no one has come to claim her. All her letters to England have been unanswered.'

That sounded suspicious indeed. Titus grimaced. The idea of being cheated out of a fortune — if he had one — seemed abhorrent. Although, it was unlikely anyone would attempt to rob a strong young man. But if he were a mere boy, or a trusting girl, then he could believe it might be easy for someone to cheat them.

He cleared his throat again, trying to ignore his throbbing wound. 'Reverend Mother, I think someone should undo this injustice.'

'And what do you suggest we do?'

We? It was quite clear to him from her stern looks, exactly who she had in mind to restore Helen Martindale's rightful inheritance. And that person was, himself!

Away would go his carefree, bachelor ways, his reckless gambling and nights of pleasure. Out of the window would fly his drinking chums and his shady dealing. He would have to learn to be respectable. He should give this wronged young lady a chance in life. Find the person responsible for her abduction and see them punished. Restore her fortune.

Titus wanted to protest th he
couldn't do it. Social life in E nd
had exacting standards. English y
was ruled by matrons who reg
everything, like generals ruled the
No-one was allowed to step out
Everyone had to obey the ru re
etiquette — even if they had a f wh
Especially if their fortune was ga in
trade, which he believed the Mar th
money was. co

It would embarrass him hav. V
bring a Spanish nun into the h
circles. She wouldn't know abou
niceties of good breeding. Talk abc
fish being thrown out of the water!

Titus gulped at the abbess's exp
ant face. He didn't want to take He
on. He shook his head slowly. No sir.

Suddenly Sister Lucia's bright, youn
face came into his mind. He realised
not only was it a duty he should do, he
had a strange niggle in his brain that he
wanted to . . .

'Well, Reverend Mother, she could be
sent to England. I'm sure my parents

d look after her — while her
ine is sought.'

h, Captain, I hoped you would say
!' Her smile looked genuine. 'You
uld understand that Sister Lucia has
taken any vows to stay here. She is
e to leave. But who will escort her
ile she travels to your parents' home
England? And with the remnants of
e French Army scattered about our
untryside after Wellington's victory at
itoria, who will be with her to protect
er?'

Titus swallowed again. He was
delighted to hear about the victory at
Vitoria, perhaps his information had
got to Sir Arthur, er, Wellington, as he
was now called. But now it seemed
clear to him that the Mother Abbess
wanted Sister Lucia to leave the
convent as much as the little nun
wanted to go. And he owed this
community of nuns a debt.

He cleared his throat. 'I am . . . an
honourable man,' he said with difficulty
because it didn't sound right. So he

added, 'I promise I will escort Helen to the coast and deliver Helen to my parents' home. Then do my best to restore her wealth.' *And put up with the scorn of my raffish friends — and the fun they will have with me trying to instruct a nun in how to behave in Society!*

The abbess smiled. 'It is not I who you have to answer for that promise, Captain, but the Lord.'

'You have my word as an English gentleman . . .' as I intend to become one, he went on in silence.

'Very well. It is unlikely that anyone else will come this way who will escort her home, or offer to look after her interests. And I believe you are a good man and will not take advantage of her . . . ?'

Titus, with a red face, stuttered, 'Of course I will not harm her. I swear it.'

'Very well, Captain.' She looked up at the crucifix on the wall. 'The Lord has heard your oath. Now let us get on with the particulars.'

It pleased him to think that the Mother Abbess — who he had now more respect for — believed he was an honourable man. It was nice to think someone had faith in him. It was a good start to his new life.

The abbess was putting the coins back into his pouch, 'You must know a few things before you go. First, the girl can be stubborn. She has a mind of her own. She will lead you a merry dance — if you let her.'

Titus's eyebrows raised. Good Lord! Taking charge of a wayward filly all the way to England was not what he had in mind. Weren't nuns supposed to be docile, and biddable? It crossed his mind it was no wonder the nuns were glad to see the back of her! And he had to take her although he was still in pain; handicapped by a sore arm; in the middle of a foreign country — and he had no money.

But the abbess ignored his look of dismay. 'Here's your money,' she said giving the pouch of money to him. 'You will need it to feed yourselves and to pay for your passage. I can give you no more, as we have none. I suggest you take a local woman with you, who wishes to travel to San Sebastian — '

'I would prefer a strong horse.'

'I daresay, but we haven't one. Now, I think you would be safer pretending to be pilgrims on The Way of St James. You have a bad arm and you can say you are going to Santiago de Compostela for a cure. You can always claim to have got lost if necessary. Then when you get to San Sebastian, which has just been won back from the French, you can take a ship to England.'

Titus looked at the nun in admiration. What more could he add? She'd thought of everything. And what good news to hear that Wellington had taken the port of San Sebastian! Thankfully the French were on the run, back over the Pyrenees to France, where they belonged. But all the more dangerous for him if he should meet any raggle-taggle end bits of the French Army.

French soldiers lived off the land. They stole food from the villagers, they were not supplied with vitals from the ships like the British, and so the French were unpopular and hungry — and hungry men could be vicious.

Perhaps he could get out of this perilous journey? He enquired hopefully, 'But will Miss Martindale agree to this plan? She will have to know that there are always dangers in any journey, and this expedition might be horrendously difficult. I dread to think what could happen . . . ' Titus was telling the truth. He was well travelled, and knew he was taking on a tremendous burden with two women, an injured arm — and a new honourable conscience to boot!

'Life is a dangerous journey, Captain. But the French have been beaten and our land is free again, thank God.'

'I fear they may not be entirely gone from this region,' he reminded her.

She glared at him. 'Enough are

defeated for Spain to gain her independence! Anyway, the war is over, and you are returning to England. So . . . ' her voice rose and he trembled, ' . . . it is just a question of whether Sister Lucia wishes to go with you. Shall I ask her?'

He was nailed. He looked down at his boots and shuffled them. Words escaped him, so he nodded.

The Mother Abbess rang a small bell by her elbow and shortly after a nun appeared. 'Yes, Mother?'

'Sister Theresa, go and find Sister Lucia and tell her she is to come to my study immediately.'

When the nun had closed the door and flitted away, Titus endeavoured to think clearly, to plan his strategy as he always did when his commander gave him a mission to accomplish. His ability to assess a situation, decide how to overcome problems and his tenacity to achieve the objective, was his strength as a military scout.

★ ★ ★

His Grace the Duke of Wellington appreciated these qualities in Captain Stonely, and had always overlooked any tittle tattle he heard about his officer's wayward behaviour.

In fact, the Commander was most upset to hear from some French captives that the Captain had been killed getting some important information to him. Which had helped his victory over the French in the Basque country.

The Duke had even found the time to write to Captain Stonely's father, the Earl of Parkham, to tell him how sorry he was to hear of Titus's death and how valuable his son had been.

4

When she heard Sister Theresa calling her, Helen stiffened. She was picking beans in the vegetable garden and was in amongst the tall, straggly plants, feeling quite content to be alone with her daydreams in the shade from the baking sun. Now it seemed she was being sought and she guessed it was for something she should or should not have done.

The Spanish nuns she lived with were kindly at heart, but their lives were ruled by a plethora of regulations imposed by the Church and over-zealous idealism. And their punishments were severe.

'I'm over here, Sister Theresa,' she called, picking up her basket of beans and sighing to be leaving such a pleasant spot. Convent life had few occasions that could be described as blissful. And although she had given a message for the English soldier to deliver when he got to England, she had the sinking feeling he might not, because in his confession she had overheard he was having an affair with her aunt.

So Aunt Caroline Sands would never hear about her incarceration in the convent, and here she would remain forever, becoming as staid as Sister Theresa who'd come to fetch her.

'Oh dear child, your pinafore is very dirty. Take it off. Mother wants you in her study. Right away.'

Helen blanched. She'd had enough telling off recently and feared what ever it was she'd done would earn her another whipping. The Spanish nuns were so keen on physical punishment thinking it cleaned the soul, but as far as Helen was concerned it was unnecessarily harsh. Nothing would make her into a perfect nun!

'What does she want this time?' Helen asked herself taking off her pinafore and shaking some earth from the hem of her long skirt.

Sister Theresa adjusted Helen's veil saying, 'I don't know, Sister Lucia, but she has that English soldier with her.'

Helen put her hands over her face. Had Reverend Mother discovered she had asked that man to deliver a message to her aunt?

Then she shrugged her slight shoulders, thinking the abbess was aware of her being discarded by her family and had allowed her to write to them, although never a word had ever got back to her.

Puzzled, Helen began to run, then stopped, as it was not permitted to run in the convent, and she walked with sprightly steps towards the abbess's study.

She put her ear to the door and heard laughter. Male and female laughter!

Flattening herself against the wall outside the study she breathed deeply. It was a shock. Laughter in recreation time was allowed, but coming from the abbess's study at midday, it was amazing!

It was that man in there. How little she knew about the male sex. How fascinated she was to learn more about men. And why shouldn't she?

She wasn't a real nun who had sworn to live in a convent. With her heart beating at a faster rate than normal, she knocked and was bidden to enter.

He was standing there. How tall he was. How handsome. The man of her dreams. After greeting her superior in the correct manner, she turned and smiled politely at the officer, but he didn't smile back.

She thought he looked more than a little put out. Perhaps his injury was giving him a great deal of pain.

'Ah, Sister Lucia, come and sit down,' Reverend Mother said. And Helen was relieved her tone suggested she wasn't in grave trouble with some convent rule.

Helen looked at the invalid and the only chair. 'Shouldn't he sit down?' she asked looking at his uneasey stance.

'Ladies have priority,' he said bowing.

And before she could say she wasn't a lady, the abbess looked at Helen keenly. 'Captain Stonely has made an offer to escort you to England and to find your family.'

Helen hid a gasp as she sat down.

'What do you think about that?'

She felt hit between the eyes. Bowled over. Completely flabbergasted! She was glad she was sitting, and for a moment or two, unable to utter a word.

Then joy struck her. 'Why, that is wonderful!' she exclaimed, clasping her hands together in rapture.

'Humph!' The Captain was looking down at his boots. 'It ain't going to be a picnic, you know. First we have to get to San Sebastian and find a ship.'

'A ship!' Helen exclaimed unable to hide her excitement. 'A real ship? To England?'

'Well, yes,' agreed Titus, wondering if the abbess had not told him that Sister Lucia was a little touched in the head.

'I'm not thinking of rowing you over the Bay of Biscay.'

'Sailing will be fun.'

Titus groaned inwardly. 'Well, it may not be fun,' he said promptly, 'the ship may be full of soldiers returning to England, and they can be a rough lot.'

The Mother Abbess interjected, 'But Captain Stonely has promised to guard you. And, if you decided to go, you must promise to obey him.'

'Of course,' Helen agreed. She was still trying to absorb the wonderful news that she was to be set free. Her daily dream to return to England was possible at last. She couldn't help smiling widely.

Titus shot a quick look at her overjoyed face and hoped that point, about being willing to be led by him, had sunk in. If she had an independent streak then it could be most awkward to control her. It could lead to dangerous situations. He knew little about controlling others, but he knew quite a lot about being troublesome to others.

He'd had a lifetime's practice.

The abbess observed the young people. Sister Lucia didn't appear reluctant to go with Captain Stonely, in fact, as the girl's bright blue eyes met his keen, grey orbs, she would have objected to that show of familiarity by one of her nuns, only Sister Lucia was Helen Martindale, a young lady who had the right to be attracted to a young man.

Yes, indeed, from what she knew of the pair they seemed very suited. And the Captain's sensible, if rather dampening, remarks about the coming journey, were to the abbess's mind, correct. But she also knew that Sister Lucia was like any youngster, full of enthusiasm and excitement to be released from confinement. Sister Lucia was far from being unintelligent. And neither, the abbess judged, was the English Captain at all dusty about the head.

'You must realise,' the abbess told Helen, 'that the Captain is taking you back to England for your benefit. The

55

journey would be difficult enough for him without taking you, but it is his kindness, his sense of justice, that makes him offer to escort you to his parents' home, and then to enquire about your family and circumstances.'

'I appreciate that,' Helen said firmly. Her expression changed and she said seriously, 'I will not forget what I owe him.'

Titus mumbled quickly, 'You will owe me nothing, Miss Martindale. I just ask, as your superior has just told you, that you keep in mind that the journey may be dangerous and difficult. At times, especially uncomfortable for you. And I will expect you to obey me during the journey.'

'Oh indeed, I will,' Helen nodded her head vigorously.

Titus sighed. He feared she was an inexperienced girl. He would much prefer to be travelling alone.

'And you will nurse his wound,' added the abbess. 'Your journey to San Sebastian may take a week or more if the weather is fine. When the rains come it will be more difficult for you, so it is better to leave soon and avoid them.'

'Yes, and there may still be an English supply ship in port for a while yet, so we may get a passage on one,' Titus said, thinking out loud.

'Four o'clock in the morning would be a good time to set out.'

'Tomorrow morning?' gulped Titus.

'In the morning,' repeated the abbess.

Titus thought it far too early. His mind was reeling to cope with the overload it had been given. He had little time to prepare himself for the physical effort and had no map to plan the best route. Or to get a gun, should they clash with some French soldiers. Then he remembered they were going to pretend to be pilgrims.

Although he had no idea what pilgrims were like. Anyway, he was glad they wouldn't be taking the abbess along with them. He would not be able to live up to her high standards, and he doubted that the excited young lady by his side would either.

The abbess stood up to dismiss them. 'Now, I want you both to leave me and think about this agreement. Visit the church and pray for guidance. Then, if you are both still willing to proceed, you must come and tell me, and you will have my blessing to go tomorrow.'

Having made her nun-like obeisance, and Titus a stiff bow, Titus opened the door for Helen to leave the abbess's study, and shut the door quietly after them.

In the corridor they looked at one another. 'Ahem,' he said.

'Shall I show you the chapel, sir?'

Titus nodded, it was as good a place as any to plan the journey. To try and remember the terrain they would have to cover.

But sitting in the little chapel, and thinking how near death he'd been a short time ago, he felt grateful. He was sure he shouldn't have refused the difficult task he'd been given. He even had a sneaking feeling he might enjoy the challenge of taking Helen back to England and solving the mystery of her banishment. He'd always been a one man band, now companionship seemed to offer some attractions.

The next morning, when the sun began to make its appearance over the Spanish hills, a sharp rap on the door awoke Titus.

Years of military training enabled him to shake off sleep — but not the throbbing pain in his shoulder and arm as he struggled into his clothes. Strange clothes that had mysteriously appeared on his chair and he guessed they were his disguise as a pilgrim. Gone were his fine leather boots and rough tie-on sandals replaced them.

His officer's breeches had vanished too and some baggy trousers and a clean, but much mended, cloak was ready for him to put on. And a wide brimmed hat, which would be useful to protect him from the sun.

There was a cloth sack too and inside he saw the nuns had put his own clothes. He had to hand it to them. Those nuns were as efficient as soldiers. But then, they did have a harsh discipline, like the army.

Coming out of the infirmary cell, he spotted Mother Abbess and a girl by her side, and marching up to them he saw it was Helen dressed in a drab, ankle-length skirt, a long-sleeved shapeless shirt, and a long shawl which covered her head and practically all the rest of her. Her little feet were covered with bandages. She also carried a small cloth bag. She looked overall like any peasant girl wearing worn clothes. But, when she turned to him, the excitement in her eyes made them as bright and sparkling as new gold coins.

'Are you ready, Captain?' enquired the abbess.

He bowed. 'Reverend Mother, Miss Martindale.'

Helen knelt for a blessing then made for the door out into the wide world.

The abbess turned to him. 'Helen has been told all I know about the circumstances about her being left here eight years ago. Which isn't much, I'm afraid. But she is keen to trace any of her relatives and I charge you to help her. Although some may not be keen to see her again.

'Now, I have a sister living in San Sebastian. I can't promise she will be able to assist you getting a passage, but I have written a letter for you to give to her. And if when you reach the coast Helen feels she wants to return to us, then leave her with my sister.'

A tiny and very old peasant woman was approaching them and was introduced as Helen's Basque-speaking female companion, Maria.

Titus, who hid his disappointment to find he'd been saddled with a lame horse as well as everything else, summoned a smile for Maria, and thanked the abbess politely.

He wished he had a horse to ride as he set off quickly. He hated long goodbyes, he tapped his foot impatiently, but was aware that the nuns appeared and wanted to shower Helen with their good wishes before she left.

And when at last the three pilgrims set off he noticed the old peasant woman walked slowly and the track down the mountain was steep and winding, so he couldn't stride ahead at his normal speed.

Helen was free. She smiled at Titus walking ahead and hoped he wouldn't forget Maria was hobbling. It was quite a steep climb down from the convent and there were only animal tracks for them to follow. But the sight of the early morning sun touching the jagged hills and the trees and shrubs, was awe-inspiring.

Helen felt glad to be alive. Her new life of freedom was beginning. She was no longer the spoilt child who had been kidnapped and brought to the convent. She was now a grown woman — and the nuns, for all their harsh ways, had taught her many useful things. Not that she hadn't more to learn from that man in front.

After half-an-hour, she wished the Captain wouldn't walk so fast. She could keep up, even wearing the bandages over her feet, which she wasn't used to wearing, but Maria was struggling, pour soul, and they had only just started their long trek.

Perhaps he was going to walk off and leave them? After an hour, Helen began to feel a little anxious. She caught glimpses of him in the distance and she was worried as Maria, she observed, was ready for a rest.

She wanted to call out to the Captain to stop charging ahead, but having had drummed into her the danger of coming across some wandering French soldiers, she didn't dare shout to him.

By mid morning, she was feeling sweaty from tramping under the hot sun for hours, tired from assisting Maria get down the stony path, and very thirsty.

All she could do was to keep going

down the mountain, hoping she was taking the right track, assisting the old woman, and holding both her own and Maria's bundle — hoping she would find the Captain again soon.

And when they came to a particularly difficult ledge with a steep drop on one side, Helen felt a trifle annoyed, as it crossed her mind that he should have assisted them on this scary, palm-dampening part. But, she told herself, he did have an injured arm, and maybe he was reconnoitring — making sure there was no dangers ahead of them.

5

Helen didn't like to hurry the old woman. She put safety first. And it was a great relief when they stepped off the winding goat track on to a flat, wider path. There they stopped for a few minutes and while her companion stood to regain her breath, Helen surveyed the green valley below with its isolated farms.

Rugged stone walls and fields showed it was inhabited. There were a few whitewashed, red-tiled houses and farm buildings. Cattle strolled, munching knee-high grass and she heard someone calling, and in the distance a dog barking.

It fascinated her to view the beautiful Basque countryside, which had been so near the remote convent, and yet had been out-of-bounds to her for years. She had come back to the world and she felt reborn.

The surge of happiness at being released from her confinement made her smile, and it was only when she felt Maria's claw-like hand tug at her sleeve that she remembered she was far away from freedom.

Where was that man she was supposed to be following?

They trudged on down the path. Suddenly ahead she saw a man waving and calling them. It was the Captain holding an old donkey.

Approaching him she could have chided him for frightening her by charging off and leaving her wondering if she would see him again, but her days of petulance were over. She had acquired maturity at the convent, a belief in forgiveness and a cheerful outlook.

'Why Captain,' she cried walking up and stroking the gentle beast's large furry head and long ears, 'We lost you.'

He smiled somewhat dryly as if he was only partly glad to see the women again. 'I don't know how you managed it, Miss Martindale, but you followed a far steeper track down than the one I took. I was wondering if I'd have to haul myself up to the convent again and report that I'd lost you within the hour of us leaving. But then I was warned you had a mind of your own and might go off on a merry dance.'

Helen gulped at his audacity, blaming her! He was at fault, walking too fast and leaving them to find the way.

Turning to Maria she asked the tiny peasant woman if she would like to ride the donkey and was assured that a ride would be most welcome.

Their pace went faster after Maria was mounted.

Several hours later, when Helen's stomach was rumbling from lack of food, they stopped near a farmhouse. Titus went on alone to see who was there.

'Come,' he beckoned from a distance and when they joined him he informed them that they were fortunate to find a farmer and his wife who would offer them hospitality overnight. If only in the hay barn.

'I'm pleased to hear that, Captain. I think Maria and the donkey have had enough and you look all in. Besides, I need to dress your wound.'

She thought they couldn't have found a better place to settle for the night. Being able to speak Basque, which Titus could not, Helen and Maria were able to talk to the farmer and his wife, which made the party welcome by their hosts who were keen to see them fed and watered — including the donkey. After a simple but sustaining meal, Maria sank on to her pallet in the sweet-smelling hay with thankful prayers and was soon asleep.

Helen dressed the Captain's wound remarking how well it was healing.

'It doesn't feel as if it is!' he grumbled.

Helen replied, 'I daresay it will pain you for some time and your long walk today has been exhausting for you,' she said sympathetically.

He muttered as he lay down on his

pallet, 'It is not the walk that bothers me, Miss Martindale, it's all the baggage I'm having to take with me!'

Insulted to be referred to as baggage, Helen pressed her lips tightly together. Now she knew exactly what he thought of her! As she lay down on the straw as far away as possible from him, she hoped she'd soon be able to remove herself for ever from the sinful man.

After all, she knew exactly what he was really like, exactly what faults he had proclaimed out loud the first time she'd met him. Under his officer-like veneer he was a very flawed man.

What was it she'd heard him confess? Disrespectful to his parents; a gambling man; a thief; frequently drunk and lustful . . .

In her opinion, Captain Stonely didn't have to pretend to be a pilgrim on the Way of St James, he needed to repent. But before she fell asleep she reminded herself that she was no angel either.

Helen was used to rising early and hearing the farm's cockerel crowing was a familiar sound for her.

Not wishing to disturb the sleeping Captain and shorten Maria's rest, Helen went out of the barn. It was a treat for her to choose to get up. There were no convent bells ringing at certain times of the day, no routine to be followed and instructions to be obeyed until it was time to go to bed again.

When she went outside she saw the fiery red streaks in the sky promising another fine day. She breathed deeply, exhilarated by the fresh mountain air.

She went to see the donkey and kissed the animal's soft muzzle saying, 'I'll have to take one step at a time, but I'll get my fortune back, or I'm not my father's daughter.

'It was his ambition, and hard work, that made him a rich merchant, and I'll be just as determined.'

Aware of someone watching her, she

turned to see the Captain propping himself up by the stable door. 'Yes indeed, Miss Martindale, I believe you will,' he said.

'Why, Captain, you startled me!'

'You have a lot to learn young lady and I suggest you start by realising I could be a French soldier looking for a romp in the hay with an unprotected girl!'

She gave a shudder. Harsh words he said, but true.

'Captain,' she turned on him saying crisply. 'It doesn't help to look on the black side. But I accept your point and will be more careful in future.' She swept by him holding her chin up. She didn't want him to see the tears in her eyes.

He'd destroyed the magical spell of the morning for her. But she was realistic enough to know her new life was going to be a mix of thrills and disappointments, fears and pains. Unpleasantness of all kinds would undoubtedly spring up and she would have to deal with it.

'I beg your pardon, Miss Martindale,' she heard him coming up behind her, 'It was unforgivable of me to have been so rag-mannered. Please accept my apologies. I am not used to being with nuns. I'll endeavour to change my uncouth ways.'

She couldn't bring herself to turn and look at him. She brushed the wetness from her eyes hurriedly. Then in a croaky voice she said, 'I understand I'm a burden to you, Captain. I assure you I will endeavour to avoid being like troublesome baggage.'

'You've shown me already you are a girl with spirit. That I admire. So dry your tears. Sure it would be easier for me not to have a painful, injured arm, and not to have two women and a donkey to take along, but that's not your fault. Besides, you speak Basque and have that advantage over me.'

He was close to her now and she quickly wiped her eyes. 'Thank you, sir,' she said with a sniff.

She heard him breathe deeply, 'I

promised your Mother Abbess to help you regain your position in English Society and that I am going to do. And I promise I'll not refer to you as *baggage* again.'

She turned to look up at his face, which was like his body, hard, lean and well-structured — yet his grey eyes seemed softer. She saw too that he was teasing her — but not unkindly — so her lips twitched. She said, 'Well sir, after being shut away in the convent I admit I don't know how to go about doing many things.'

'I can't tell you how I think you should act, young lady. You'll have to make those decisions for yourself as we proceed. But I will, of course, advise you.'

They were now looking at each other as friends. Helen feeling apprehensive, yet more confident that he genuinely cared and would help her.

He smiled as his fingers came to stroke a curl of her hair, 'Your hair needs to grow longer.'

Embarrassed to have forgotten to put on her veil when she got up, Helen frowned.

'Oh, don't worry about it, Miss Martindale, I believe by the time you reach England you will have a mane as long as the donkey's!' He smiled suddenly, 'Your hair is a beautiful golden colour.'

It was nice to be flattered. She patted her hair thinking how the nuns hacked it short, not caring for its looks, because it was hidden under a veil. But she remembered as a child her nursemaid brushing her long hair and saying she was lucky to have such lovely hair.

'Well sir, my hair is one thing I'm not going to worry about. But, to go to the other end of me, my feet are a concern, with far more walking to do.'

His eyes looked down at her feet. 'Let me look at them.'

Despite the bandages that had covered her feet yesterday her feet felt raw underneath. She sat by the well to examine the soles of her feet.

'My goodness,' he exclaimed kneeling by her and examining her beautifully-formed feet, 'We must find you some shoes.'

The feel of his long fingers on her feet shot a strange sensation through her body. He cradled her foot tenderly as if he was holding a dove, gently stroking the creamy softness of her skin. Like a soothing balm his touch was quite the most beautiful feeling she'd ever experienced. She looked up into his eyes and noticed that they were beautiful too.

Lost in sensual feelings she couldn't understand, Helen felt the delightful warmth of security, realised that the Captain would do her no harm. For all his rough words, he did seem to care about her.

The farmer's wife produced some well-worn Basque slippers which tied up the calves for Helen to wear. She didn't like to say how difficult she found it to wear shoes but, having the ointment for the Captain's wound, she used some of that on her blisters and bound up her feet in thin bandages to act as stockings.

After breakfasting on eggs and bread, the party set off again. The donkey having acquired a halter was easy to lead. Maria seemed happy perched on its back and Titus was able to walk abreast with Helen as the path became wider.

They walked in silence for a while, then Titus explained, 'As a scout I have to concentrate on the sights and sounds ahead and behind me. Be ready to dob behind a bush should I encounter anyone, who might be friend or foe.'

'I regret we are an added trouble for you.'

He turned and smiled down at her. 'Well, you are — and you aren't, Miss Martindale.

Her face adopted a curious look. 'What do you mean by that?'

The donkey snorted as it clip-clopped along by fragrant pine and beech trees. 'I appreciate your company, ma'am. Indeed

I admire your quietness, you don't chatter endlessly or complain like most women I've known.'

'Oh, but I do complain. It's just that you can't hear it!'

He chuckled. She was pleased he had a sense of humour.

They continued their journey along narrow roads by high summer pastures, where sheep grazed peacefully. She longed to question him about his boyhood, his family and his friends. She wondered what he enjoyed doing, hunting, or sailing or gaming, ah yes, he'd admitted he like gaming and drinking a little too much!

6

Having climbed down one mountain, Helen saw others blocking their way and the walk became uphill, then downhill again. She began to wonder if they would ever reach San Sebastian.

Helen had time to reflect and wonder if she would fit into English life. She asked herself, what did she really want out of life — apart from regaining her fortune?

One day, as she rode along on the donkey, Maria said sadly, 'My man died a few months back. I can't manage to live alone in the mountains in the wintertime. Our son was killed fighting the French, so I had to give our farm to relatives. I'm going to live with my daughter in Bilbao, which is along the coast, not far from San Sebastian. I'll miss the farm animals and the mountains . . . ' her voice trailed off, she was clearly upset.

Helen felt for her and said with a sigh, 'Maria, you, like me, have the difficulty of adjusting to a new way of life.'

'Ah, but you are young, my dear. You will marry and have children.'

Helen smiled wryly. 'I'm not young enough, or attractive, to find a husband.'

'Oh, but you are. The Captain thinks so.'

Surprised to think the Captain even bothered to think about her, as he always appeared to be concentrating on the road ahead, Helen blushed.

Suddenly she was aware Titus had stopped walking. 'God knows what we are going to do!' she heard him exclaim as they approached a village. 'I spy some French soldiers ahead.'

Indeed it was a dilemma. Made worse because the man who was supposed to protect them, and had done his best to do so, now seemed at a loss what to do.

Helen knew she had to think of

something quickly. 'Captain!' she called.

His eyes swivelled around hearing her urgent call.

'Remember we are pilgrims. Act like a beggar. Give me your sack with your uniform in and Maria can sit on it like a saddle on the donkey.'

To her amazement he obeyed her.

'Captain,' she said again, 'we have some red berries we picked with us. I suggest we crush some, and cover our faces with the dabs of red dye until we look spotty, then we can tell the soldiers not to come near us as we have a disease, and are going to Santiago de Compostela to pray to St James for a cure.'

'Very well, it's worth a try,' she heard him mutter.

The red juice was made hurriedly and they quickly painted their faces.

'The juice spots look most effective. I would say you are suffering from something — even though I couldn't say what it might be!' she quipped and received a tight smile in return.

The ruse worked and they were able to pass by the village without mishap.

Titus grinned at Helen. 'That was well done, Miss Martindale. Well done, indeed, for you to think up such a scheme so quickly. And to keep your head. I was afraid you might have had the vapours.'

Helen blushed under his praise. 'Vapours were not encouraged at the convent, Captain. It was just good fortune we had the berries,' she said modestly.

His eyes sought hers. 'Maybe, ma'am. But I'm proud of you.'

Helen felt overjoyed to think she had earned his approval. She wasn't sure why it meant so much to her. She felt safe in his company, but realised he, like her, was vulnerable at times and was glad of assistance.

There was an excitement about being on the pilgrim path. Helen felt it keenly. The ancient way, signposted by scallop shells — which was useful for those who couldn't read — made her think of medieval travellers who were she thought not unlike themselves on a quest. 'Thousands of pilgrims have been trudging this path for centuries to pray at the Shrine of Saint James,' she remarked to the Captain, who had become more talkative of late.

'Indeed. Only they were going another way!' he remarked with a grin. He stood and looked up at a huge stone cross on the Camino, that marked the pilgrims' way, 'The great cathedrals of Burgos, Leon and Santiago, which I've been fortunate to see, were built by the fervour and money of the pilgrims.'

'It's a shame we're not going to Santiago.'

Titus turned to look at Helen's wistful face. He looked along the pilgrims' road, far away in the distance, as if he were looking into the future. 'We have a purpose however. I'm starting a new life to try and correct my youthful follies. I intend to heal the rift with my father, and show I can be a worthy gentleman — '

'Worthiness sounds a little dull, sir. I prefer you just as you are.'

He chuckled. 'Don't concern yourself that I will achieve much!' Then he looked at her as he continued, 'And you are going to attain your proper status as a refined and elegant lady.'

'Do you think that is possible?'

'Well,' he said stepping away from her, rubbing the stubble on his chin, while looking at her nun-like garments. 'I'm sure it won't be difficult for you to make a little improvement . . .'

She looked at his twinkling eyes and laughed merrily. 'I'm sure you are right about that.'

He smiled reassuringly. 'No, I shouldn't tease you, Miss Martindale. I believe you should be reinstated. It's not right that someone has stolen your worldly goods, and they should be dealt with. And I should help you. Your affairs must be set right.'

Helen nodded, she was gratified to think he saw their goals as something noble and correct to do. And it was, she thought, very kind of him to entwine his aspiration with hers.

When they eventually arrived at the outskirts of San Sebastian, and saw the sea in the distance, they were no longer afraid of being accosted by any remnants of the French army.

The Captain shaved and had changed into his own clothes by the next morning. Helen could barely keep her eyes off him smartened up. His repaired jacket was dark green, showing he was an officer in the Rifle Corps. He didn't sport the bright red coat with richly embroidered gold or silver lace that most British officers wore.

She noted the fine quality of the details of his dress: the standing collar and cuffs of black velvet, and the plated buttons held in place with black silk twist. His trousers were well worn, to an almost black colour, yet it was the exact fit to his muscled legs that Helen admired.

His riding boots looked clean, but the nuns lacked the polish to make them shine. Long ago he must have lost his hat, but his long curled hair was combed in order.

But Helen's thoughts soon turned to other worries. Approaching the town she noticed the people they met turned to stare disapprovingly in their direction. She had to concede her party probably did look odd. Even the Captain seemed concerned to be the object of curiosity. He whispered to Helen, 'I detect some hostility in the people's eyes. I wonder why that is?'

Helen wondered if it may be because she might look like a nun walking with a handsome young officer, which they may have judged to be the wrong thing to do. Or that the poor old donkey, way past its best years, was being made to carry an old woman.

Gazing over the low, sandy peninsular, to the town of San Sebastian, which was dominated by a castle, they could see a disaster had occurred.

'Why the place has been torched!' declared the Captain in horror.

Helen could see a fire had burned much of the small town centre. Coming closer, they could see even more of a tragedy had occurred. The place had been ransacked. The town was in ruins. The townsfolk that were about were pitiful to see.

'Oh, my God!' breathed Titus, his voice catching, in anger. 'It's like Badajoz, all over again. The British troops have stormed the town. Behaved like . . . like savage animals!'

Helen was horrified to see the devastation. To smell the acrid smell that still hung in the air. After a few minutes, she felt him take her hand. 'I can offer no excuse for this carnage. Indeed it makes me sad to think I had anything to do with the British army when I see what they have done. But you should understand that war is evil — millions have suffered since Napoleon invaded Spain and Portugal. Men, women, child and beast, have been injured and died.'

'But did the British do this monstrous

harm to the townsfolk?' asked Helen in a strained voice.

'I can only think that our troops suffered heavy losses on breaching the town's defences, and then acted in revenge.' He breathed in sharply and shook his head as he let out his breath again, and sighed. 'It's dreadful. Shameful! I don't believe Wellington would have given the order to sack the town.'

The Captain released her hand saying, 'I think we must try and find the house where the Abbess's sister lives, and hope it is not destroyed. Look for the street signs,' giving Helen a task to help take her mind off the devastation.

Helen began to wonder what Senora Clara Moran, the Abbess's sister, would be like. And would she — was she able — to help them, especially now after the plunder of San Sebastian?

7

The house they had stopped in front of was a splendid Basque villa, with an air of wealth about it. The garden's heavy ornate gates were firmly locked and the huge windows shuttered.

'If this is the Senora Moran's house, I'd better go and see if she is there,' the Captain said, tying the donkey's halter to the railings outside.

The way he jumped up to grasp the top of the railings then heaved his body up to strike his leg over the railings, made Helen gasp. Then she stood wide-eyed in admiration at his leap to the other side, thinking his injured arm might hurt him.

'Bravo!' she called clapping her hands, and he turned briefly and grinned.

He trod warily towards the great house. And then he disappeared into the shrubbery. Helen and Maria peered through the railings waiting, listening for him to return. What on earth would they do if he didn't?

Later, he strode up to the railings and spoke through the bars. 'The Senora is safe — although the house has suffered after being broken into. A servant is bringing the gate keys.'

Sure enough it wasn't long before an elderly servant appeared and let them into the house grounds. 'He says we are welcome,' Helen translated his Basque greeting.

A little later, the Spanish lady who came down the great staircase to greet them, reminded Helen, for a moment or two, of the Mother Abbess. She possessed the same build and facial features, but she appeared frailer. But then, Helen remembered, the lady had suffered in the siege and sacking of her town.

Titus gave her a formal bow, and Helen curtsied. Maria sat on a chair nearby. The lady of the house greeted them graciously. 'I thank you for bringing the letter from my sister. I will help you as far as I am able to, but as you are aware you have arrived at a tragic time for the people of San Sebastian.' She looked around with black, sad eyes at her wrecked home.

'We shouldn't have bothered you, Senora. We are deeply sorry for the hurt the British have influenced on you.'

Her long black eyelashes closed over her eyes. She gave a slight tremble before she looked at them again. 'It was not only the British troops who came to San Sebastian and harmed us,' she explained. 'The French invaded our country. They have harmed us far more.' She gave a sigh. 'And now the British have got rid of them, and Spain will lick its wounds and rebuild.'

'Senora, is there anything I can do for you?' enquired Titus.

She shook her head and then looked at Helen's rags. 'I can see it is I who needs to assist you — as much as I can.'

And indeed the lady of the house

offered all she could. Accommodation, meagre rations of food, helped by the fresh cheeses and wine the Captain had wisely insisted they carried in case no hospitality was available. Fruit was readily available to be harvested in the garden: lush peaches and plums. They sat down to a meal that evening in shabby grandeur.

Senora Clara Moran explained, 'My sister and I joined the convent in the mountains as young girls. I think I was persuaded by her fervour for the religious life. But my health is not robust. Before I took my vows, I decided to leave the convent. I felt unable to cope with the hard life there. My sister, the Abbess, is a dedicated nun, a strong woman, but I am not. So I got married . . . ' her voice faltered, 'my husband was killed in the recent fighting. Maybe that is God's judgment on me for refusing to serve him as a nun — '

'Dear me, no!' cried Helen. 'Reverend Mother never suggested you had failed. She appreciated you were not suited to that life. As indeed I was not. But it was not because of my health that I left, as you know . . . '

The lady smiled at her and nodded. 'You were ill done by, my sister wrote about you, and have to return to England to find your family. And, I think, you have a fine upstanding young man here to help you. You couldn't have anyone better.'

Titus gulped on his wine. To take her mind off his spluttering, Helen said quickly, 'There are many ways to live a good life, ma'am.'

The Senora smiled at her warmly. 'Yes, you are correct, my dear.'

'Do you know of any English ships in the harbour?' Titus asked.

She shook her head. 'You will have to go down and see for yourself. Ladies here do not feel safe to go out on their own.'

'Very wise, ma'am. Now if you will excuse me, I'll trot down to the harbour and see what is there.'

He rose, bowed, and made for the door. Helen thought that if she had not known he was near death a few weeks ago no-one would guess he'd been injured. He was as quick moving and supple as a fit man.

The Senora turned to Helen when he had gone. 'You'll need to get out of those nuns' drabs and put on some ladies' clothes. Let's go upstairs and see what I can find for you.' And as they began to climb the staircase she said, 'My maid was terrified and went back to her village last month. I'm hoping she'll come back to me when she's had time to overcome this.'

Helen felt she could now discuss anything with her. 'Ma'am,' she ventured to explain about Maria's need. 'The old lady who came with us is a widow and needs to get to her family in Bilbao.'

'That can be arranged. I'll find you another maid to accompany you home.'

'Maria asks if she may keep the old donkey. She's grown fond of it.'

'That too is possible. Now here's my bedchamber, let's see what I have in my closet. There is not much after the soldiers came and savagely rummaged through my belongings and took the few valuable jewels my husband gave me.'

Helen swallowed, 'How dreadful!'

'It is hard to bear when such a disaster strikes you in life — but I don't have to tell you that!'

'No, indeed, ma'am,' Helen gave a little laugh. 'And I, like you, am determined not to be bitter or seek revenge. I want to go to England and search for what is mine, but I am not intending to let it spoil the rest of my life, even if I am unsuccessful.'

The Senora smiled at her. She had read what her sister, the Reverend Mother, had written about the slender young woman before her. It was most flattering, and had Helen known about it she would have blushed.

The letter stated that the Abbess considered Miss Martindale to have attained a mature mind, that she showed a cheerful and unselfish nature — and a determination for justice any criminal should beware of!

As Titus strode down to the port of San Sebastian he wished he had some money in his pocket. Most of it had gone paying for the food they bought on the journey to the coast. But he was heartened to see masts silhouetted against the skyline.

At the harbour, he found he was amongst English-speaking men again. He noticed some idle, red-coated soldiers, and looking at them carefully he observed they were war wounded.

Waiting to be taken by boat to the three biggest ships in the harbour, flying the British Union Jack. Two of which were merchant-ships. One a huge man-of-war.

He saw a boat being rowed, it contained barrels, obviously vitals for the British army, now he guessed chasing the French over the Pyrenees Mountains. And he noticed that when the boat was unloaded, some injured soldiers were helped into the empty boat and rowed back to the ship, all with typical naval efficiency.

Titus wandered along the harbour, his task was to try and get a passage home and the boat taking the wounded was obviously the one to try.

'Can you give me a passage to England?' he asked as he approached the young naval lieutenant in charge of the boat.

The officer eyed him suspiciously. 'You'll have to ask the Commodore, sir. This ship is taking the wounded home, sir.'

Titus grimaced, then unbuttoned his jacket and took it off. Off came his shirt, to the embarrassment of the lieutenant. His bandaged shoulder and upper arm was exposed. 'Do you want me to take the bandage off lad and show you the French bullet wound, eh?'

Men had gathered around Titus to watch him strip and expose his wound. 'No, no, sir,' stuttered the lad, who had turned as bright a colour as the soldier's red coats.

Suddenly a gruff voice demanded, 'What is going on here?'

A senior naval officer had pushed by the onlookers and was staring, and blinking hard at Titus. 'Good God, Captain Stonely! We were told you were dead!'

Titus turned to look at the stout officer, recognising his high rank, 'Commodore Gilbert,' he bowed. 'Indeed I was shot, but I'm mending. I request a passage home.'

Commodore Basil Gilbert, who had known Titus as a nipper at school, picked up his friend's shirt and jacket and helped him dress again. 'I daresay I can find you a small locker.'

'And one for a lady?'

'We don't take women.'

Titus went up to him and whispered, 'She is a lady, sir. She needs your gallant assistance to get home, Basil.'

Having persuaded Commodore Gilbert to provide accommodation for himself and Helen, Titus then asked, 'When do you sail?'

'Tomorrow early with the tide. And don't expect me to wait for you. The gang plank will be hauled up and we'll sail without you if you're late.'

As Commodore Gilbert walked away he suddenly stopped and turned to Titus. 'What is the name of this, er lady?'

'Miss Helen Martindale.'

'Martindale? The missing heiress? My, oh my! Now I understand. You've found yourself a Golden Dolly!'

Titus gave a shudder. It had never occurred to him that the wealthy young lady he was escorting home would be regarded by that name. For, a Golden Dolly, was the name given to the daughter of a wealthy tradesman, who could be married and provide money for an impoverished nobleman. And Titus, who had been cut off without a penny by his father, Earl Parkham, owing to his past misdeeds, was indeed impoverished — as everyone in English Society knew.

During the hours on board ship, sailing for England, Titus suffered from acute anxiety about his almost empty purse. What he was going to do about it, he just couldn't think. He kept worrying about how he was going to get Helen into his mother's safe keeping. He knew he wasn't welcome in his father's house — or the great estate it was.

He had cooked his goose long ago. His father, the Earl of Parkham, having paid his last enormous debt, had said he never wanted to see his son again. And Titus could well understand his father's anger.

The passage home had cost him nothing as Commodore Gilbert had taken him on board as a war casualty — with his *baggage*. Helen was only too aware that she appeared as *baggage*, an unattractively-clad woman in the Senora's old clothes with a mantilla to hide her chopped hair. And having a foreign maid made her seem odd too.

The ship was returning to Plymouth,

and Titus was well aware that once on Plymouth Hoe, with the two women, they would be aware that the summer had departed and the fresh winds and squalls of early autumn would make the party in need of accommodation and a sustaining meal.

Well, desperate measures required desperate means. Titus could only think of one way to make money fast: gambling! Oh it was risky, very risky, but what else could he do?

So when the ship docked, he installed Helen and her maid at an inn, and that night made off to a gaming table.

Plymouth was full of returning officers discharged after the war, with pay packets and hoping to increase the amount in them.

The establishment Titus chose was a famous local gaming hall. Betting was in full swing. With a few shillings in his pocket Titus had to start the evening with modest wagers.

His experience, being a frequent gambler in past years, had taught him a few tricks, he had also acquired some sound knowledge of human nature, which stood him ahead of most players who only had eyes for the spinning wheel, or the next card to be revealed.

The upcome was, that in the early hours of the morning, The Honourable Titus Stonely, had not only won enough money to give the ladies a good breakfast, lunch and afternoon tea, he had acquired enough to pay for three coach fares as far as Parkham Court. And he had a thousand pounds left in his pocket!

And, needless to say, he was very happy about it. That was, until Helen got to hear about it, because he couldn't refrain from crowing about his good luck!

'I understood you had given up your raffish ways,' she said with asperity.

Titus recoiled under her stare. 'It takes time to cast off bad habits.'

'Fiddlesticks!'

Titus came up to her very close and whispered in her ear, 'Just be thankful we can now take the coach and don't have to walk all the way to London. For I hadn't enough to pay for the breakfast you've just eaten before I won some money.'

'Oh!' Helen looked up at him, 'Well,' she gradually smiled. 'In that case, I suppose we will have to make some allowances before we are set on the straight and narrow!'

'Indeed we do,' he said with a grin, thinking, heaven knows what he may need to do to discover what had happened to her home and fortune. And as the Mother Abbess had surmised, evil had been involved in Helen's abduction, then he would have to fight it by any means he could — even being a little underhand at times.

On reaching the village near Parkham Court, he installed the women in the Hungry Fox Inn, and walked up the mile-long drive to his noble father's mansion, praying his father would let his prodigal son in, and that his mama would assist Helen.

Before Titus had reached the end of the long drive, he felt overjoyed to be alive and have memories of the great house flood back. Chuckling at the childhood pranks he'd played with his brother, Charles. Forcibly reminded of how privileged he'd been as a young-ster, after weeks of travelling as a poor man. He'd taken his comfortable home, his good education, and kindly parents for granted.

He went over the contrite speech he was going to make to his father, if he was permitted to see him — and the request he was going to ask his mother — a hundred times.

In front of the great house's main entrance Titus found himself shaking like one of the falling autumn leaves. He had to tell himself firmly to get a grip.

He was an expert military scout, used to moving in and out of difficult areas without being seen. In fact the French, he knew, called members of his rifle brigade, *Grasshoppers*. So, Titus hopped around to the back of the house and cautiously let himself into the steamy, food-smelling kitchen, thankful to hear the servants laughing and talking as they partook their meal in the servants' dining hall, and didn't notice him.

He galloped up the servants' narrow, winding staircase, hoping he wouldn't meet anyone. His lordship's valet, Thornton, was a particularly burly man he'd plagued as a boy, and on seeing Titus, might well throw him out. Fortunately, he saw no-one.

The Earl of Parkham was having his after dinner nap when Titus tapped on his shiny mahogany door. His lordship's snores ceased abruptly on hearing the polite knocking, and he awoke spluttering, 'What the devil are you disturbing me for at this time, Thornton? You know I like to have five minutes snooze after my meal.'

Titus opened the door and seeing his venerable father seated in a comfortable wing chair, he came in, and bowed respectfully.

The earl grasped the chair arms tightly and blinked rapidly at his son. 'Titus!' He made a gurgling splutter, 'Am I dreaming? I thought . . .

Seeing his father was too overcome by the fact that he was standing there, alive, to say any more — and certainly the earl didn't shout at him to get out, Titus waited for a minute for the old man to recover from the shock. Then, he said humbly, 'Father I have come to apologise for my past foolish behaviour.'

The Earl of Parkham sat up straight. 'I'd never have thought it a few years ago, Titus, but I'm glad to see you, my boy. And so will your mother be. Very glad the French didn't eat you after all!'

Titus's mouth lifted a little at the corners. 'Thank you, Papa. In future I intend from now on to try and make you proud of me.'

The Earl of Parkham smiled at his son. 'But you have done already!' he said, and he did seem overjoyed. 'I received a letter a month ago from The

Duke of Wellington himself, to say he had lost a brave officer, my youngest son, Captain Titus Stonely. He thought you'd been killed, d'you see? What's more, Wellington considered you to have been valuable for gaining information about the enemy.

'Essential for the success of the Peninsular campaign! He was one of my best scouts, he wrote about you. Slippery as an eel behind enemy lines, I relied on your son, Captain Stonely, to get the information I needed. The Duke wrote, Titus never let me down.' His lordship thumped his hands on his chair arms and growled, 'Now, that, my son, made me exceedingly proud of you.'

It was Titus who now blinked rapidly. 'Well I never!' he exclaimed.

'What do you mean saying, well I never! It's true. Isn't it?'

'Papa, I was referring to my surprise of hearing you refer to Wellington as a Duke. Every time I hear of him lately, he has been promoted!'

The earl broke into laughter shaking his grey locks. 'You always were a wag, Titus.'

Titus became serious. 'I do intend to reform, sir.'

'I don't know that you need to, my boy!'

The Earl rose from his chair slowly, muttering about his stiff legs, and walked over to his polished walnut bureau. Finding a key, he unlocked a small drawer, and drew out a crackly paper letter and a two inch gleaming gold cross. Then going over to Titus, he handed him the gold medal. 'This is yours. The Duke of Wellington has awarded you this Peninsular Medal. Posthumously.'

Titus accepted the heavy gold cross, saying, 'All the officers were awarded Peninsular Medals, father.'

'Ah, but not a Cross. That's for the best of the best.'

Titus was overwhelmed. It seemed pointless to argue, that he'd only done his duty. And that he'd been fortunate on many occasions. Rash, very often — but lucky.

His father crossed the room and hugged his son. Then broke away and said in a strained voice, 'And now you are, my heir, Titus. And how glad I am our title will not pass to your cousin, for he's a stupid ass.'

Titus stood rigid. Aghast. His mind reeling. Taking in the blow that his beloved older brother had died in his absence. 'Are you telling me, my brother, Charles, is dead?'

'Yes, he was taken very ill last month . . . ' not hiding his tears, the earl slumped back in his chair and sobbed. Then stood up and walked to the long window overlooking the park. A minute later he shook off his grief and turned to Titus and said, 'Your brother, Charles, and I, will expect you to live honourably with his title, Viscount Farringdon, which is now yours.'

8

Helen revelled at being back in England. She had a permanent smile on her face as she felt the refreshing breeze. She recognised oak, elm and beech trees, whose leaves had turned to red, russet and golden colours in the sunlight. And she enjoyed watching the swallows and martins swooping over a sky filled with huge puffy clouds. The softly-formed hills, green fields and copses of trees were the landscape she remembered from long ago, and it thrilled her.

Delicious smells were wafting up from the kitchens below her inn room, where succulent smells of roast beef and fruit pies were being prepared. It was a pleasant memory of her childhood meals.

She was free! Able to look out on the stables at the back of the inn and watch the horses being tended by the ostlers for as long as she liked, without being summoned to go anywhere, or do some task, as she used to be at the sound of the convent's constantly donging bells.

Suddenly she heard hooves clattering on the cobbles and a fine horse approached the inn stable at speed. The experienced rider leapt off his steed as Helen bent out of the bedchamber window to view this expert horseman.

He looked a fine gentleman too, and he held himself well, as he threw the reigns over the horse's head, to give the leads to a groom who'd come running out to take the animal from the rider.

'M'lord,' she heard the man say, pulling his forelock. When he turned to enter the inn Helen's hand went to her bosom, as her sapphire eyes stared in a most unladylike manner, for the top-notch gentleman was Captain Stonely.

Helen flew downstairs and met him in the parlour. 'Why sir,' she cried, 'I didn't recognise you.' She needn't have asked, his happy expression told her, but she enquired, 'Did all go well?'

He nodded and replied, 'The prodigal son was received with open arms.' Then he took her hands, 'I apologise for leaving you alone for so long. Did you have lunch? You have, good, then I'll order drinks because I've much to tell you.'

He ordered a dish of coffee for Helen and a beer for himself and they seated themselves in the snug. He proceeded to tell her about his reconciliation with his parents and the sad news of the death of his brother and that consequently he was now Viscount Farringdon.

'I'm pleased for you.' She smiled at him.

'I've good news for you too, Helen. Mama will be delighted to accept you as a guest — until I find your fortune.'

'You mean, we hope to find my fortune,' she said. Her face lost its smile.

'Helen. I promised Mother Abbess I would restore your fortune and property and that is what I intend to do,' he said firmly. 'And I want to see you happily married too,' he added, wondering how many fortune hunters would soon be after the Golden Dolly until she found a husband.

She thought it kind of him to be so optimistic about her marriage prospects but only she knew how hopeless marriage was for her because there was only one man she loved, and Viscount Farringdon was not showing any signs of loving her. Besides, he was now a high-ranking lord and she was a nobody.

'Ah, I think I hear a carriage outside,' he said and drained his glass of beer. 'I've arranged to have you and your maid collected and taken up to the Hall this afternoon. I trust you are ready to meet my mama and papa?'

Helen was surprised he'd arranged this swift move for them, but smiled. 'I'm looking forward to meeting your parents,' she said, although daunted by the thought of meeting the Earl and Countess.

There was no need for her to be frightened at being suddenly moved into the polite world. She was an heiress — although at present penniless — and she didn't intend to behave as if she was in disgrace because she'd suffered the misfortune of being abducted and her fortune stolen.

Titus intended to pursue the whereabouts of Helen's fortune as soon as he had adjusted to his new position and responsibilities as Viscount Farringdon. However, he soon found there was more to do than he had anticipated. He had to familiarise himself with the Parkham house and estate affairs, which had always been his older brother's duty, and the Earl of Parkham, having reached the age of retirement, wanted Titus to take over the reins and encouraged him to do so from the first day he arrived home.

'I can see why my brother, Charles, never got into mischief — he never had the time!' Titus remarked to the estate manager.

'Nor the inclination, my lord!' retorted the manager. But he grinned, because like the rest of the house servants and estate staff, they were glad to see Titus, the wild boy, back from the wars a hero and a changed man. Titus was already showing he was going to be — much to everyone's relief and amazement — a capable heir and a caring master.

The Earl and Countess of Parkham had discussed Helen's situation with her as soon as she arrived at their home. The kindly countess had decided the first priority was that Helen should adopt the dress and manners of fashionable life, otherwise the young lady might be seen as an oddity and not able to enjoy her life in Society as an heiress, when her fortune was restored.

During the following weeks Helen was transformed into an elegant young lady. Her Spanish maid had been amply rewarded and sent back to San Sebastian carrying letters from Helen for the Reverend Mother and Senora Moran.

It was her new and expert lady's maid who now styled Helen's now long blonde hair so beautifully and dressed her in becoming floral muslin gowns. So, looking attractive — and Helen had to admit her looking glass couldn't lie — she couldn't understand why Titus seemed to keep his distance from her.

Agitated she asked his mother one breakfast time. Her ladyship leant over and patted Helen's hand, 'Don't underestimate Titus, Miss Martindale. Everyone did — but the Duke of Wellington — when he was younger. But I know he has a heart of gold.'

'That may be.' Helen frowned, feeling she should be doing something. Then she retorted, 'But he hasn't done anything about all the information I gave him about my childhood home, has he?'

The countess smiled at Helen's cross face. 'I wouldn't be surprised if he's got things moving behind scenes. Be patient, my dear. You've done very well so far learning to be an Englishwoman again. You'll soon be thrust into Society and knowing the etiquette will make you feel comfortable and able to concentrate on establishing your position.'

It was difficult to be patient, but Helen respected the kindly countess and so she had to wait until one day Titus came with news. 'I've been in contact with a firm of lawyers who hold your Grandfather Martindale's will. And I've obtained your maternal grandmother's address. Regretfully she's now old and blind — but she should remember you when you visit her.'

Helen was delighted to hear her grandmother was still alive and said so.

'Now, as to the lawyer who dealt with your father's estate, he told me of an unusual stipulation in your parents will . . .'

Helen braced herself. 'What was it?'

'Well, apart from your blind grandmamma, your mother's sister, Lady Caroline Sands . . . ' his face became a little coloured and Helen knew why.

Titus gave a little cough and continued, 'was the nearest relative on your death. Therefore, as you were missing for years, presumed dead, your property was inherited by her. But, as she is married to Lord Rodney Sands, he, in effect, has charge of it.'

Helen gave a shudder as several things she'd forgotten about her Uncle Rodney came back to her. Her Aunt Caroline, she recollected, wouldn't say boo to a goose, so it was likely her uncle took everything he wanted from his wife.

Titus confirmed what Helen knew by saying, 'Lord Sands is an overbearing and quarrelsome fellow and was not liked by Mr Martindale.' Titus took a long breath in, 'And so, Mr Martindale put in his will that Lord Sands was not to be his daughter's guardian. He appointed a bishop instead.'

'A bishop?'

'Yes, the Bishop of Truro. A worthy old gentleman, but I gather he hadn't much punch.'

'Oh yes, I vaguely remember a white-haired clergyman. An old friend of my father.'

'I'm sorry to have to tell you he went to heaven some time ago, therefore, you were left without protection.'

Helen blinked fast. 'So, my Uncle Rodney had my estate.'

'He has. And he will have to return it to you, but you must bear in mind that it was not his fault you disappeared.'

Helen squeezed her eyes shut in silent prayer. She was relieved to think her estate would now be returned to her, but she didn't relish the having to meet her Uncle Rodney, and as her aunt, Caroline, Lady Sands, had had an affair with Titus — that would be a most ticklish situation to deal with. Helen realised that getting her fortune back still might not be straightforward.

Titus waited for Helen's full attention before he continued, 'A witness needs to accompany you when you visit your grandmother and meet other people who may remember you.

118

'Because it's essential we have proof of your identity, for the law, in case Lord Sands becomes awkward and does not want to relinquish your fortune and claims you are an impostor, and if one or more people still wish to harm you, you may need a fighter by your side.'

'You are my knight in shining armour.'

Titus gave a laugh, but Helen believed it — and knew she must fight too. Titus could give no information about the person, or persons, who might have robbed her. He did say, 'What your father feared, happened, so we know there are guilty ones about.' He looked at her sadly. 'Unfortunately, it may be impossible to find the person, or persons, who wickedly abducted you as a child.'

That may be true, thought Helen, nevertheless she was not going to be put off doing her utmost to find who had harmed her and she now felt ready for the hunt to start.

9

It hadn't occurred to Helen before that it might be painful to recall parts of her childhood, but as she began to feel apprehensive she knew she must master her feelings. Only she could lead the way and find the truth about her past. However, she was grateful when Titus and his mother said they would accompany her to her grandmother's residence on the outskirts of Oxford.

She found the house was large, but small compared to the splendour of Parkham Court. It was the home of a successful businessman, which Helen's grandfather had been. Titus informed the ladies as they set off on the journey that Mr Featherstonhaugh had made a good living from banking in Oxford.

He had two daughters, one married Sir Rodney Sands and the other was Helen's mama, whose husband had made an enormous fortune as a jeweller.

Helen felt her heart hammer and a dryness in her throat as the coach slowed down in front of the house entrance. To be meeting her grandmother after so many years now seemed an ordeal. Many questions bombarded Helen. Why hadn't the old lady answered the letters she had sent her from Spain? Was it just because the lady was blind — or had someone prevented her from receiving them?

Helen was glad to find her grandmother had loyal servants who were looking after her.

The upstairs room they were shown into was large, grandly decorated and filled with quality furniture. The surroundings made the old lady, who sat shrivelled in shawls in a wing chair, look tiny.

Helen's stomach churned seeing her. She felt herself short of breath and made herself breath slowly and deeply because somewhere deep in her brain

121

she knew immediately that the lady was truly her grandmother. Kneeling at her feet, Helen gently kissed her grand-mamma's sunken cheek.

'I'm your granddaughter, Helen,' she said softly.

'They told me Helen died,' the old lady said, lifting her hand to touch Helen's face. Her dry, bony fingers felt Helen's features but no smile of loving recognition formed on the thin lips.

'I went abroad,' Helen said.

'Helen is dead. I was told she had died,' repeated the old lady stubbornly.

Helen had the sense not to argue. Instead she used the opportunity to have her memory jogged about other people she'd known years ago. 'Do you know where Helen's governess now lives?'

'Ah, the governess. Miss Picket . . . '

Delighted to have the name of her governess mentioned, and all the memories that name brought, Helen waited, but no further information was forthcoming. The old lady had nodded asleep. Helen was disappointed, but had to leave.

'Come Helen, I'll show you around Oxford,' said Titus brightly. 'The colleges are well worth looking at, and as you like plants, a visit to the Botanical Gardens should interest you.'

She felt he was being kind, trying to distract her from the uselessness of visiting her grandmother, who had not acknowledged her.

When Helen and Titus were alone, strolling amongst the shrubs, herbs, flowers and autumnal scents of the Botanical Gardens, the conversation turned to Helen's search for her roots.

Titus asked, 'Did you notice your grandmamma had a miniature of her two daughters on her mantelshelf? And one of the girls looked exactly like you?' He took the double miniature out of his pocket and put it in front of Helen's eyes.

Helen marvelled at him having it and her likeness to her mother startled her. 'My mama,' she breathed gazing at the image, which crowded her mind with loving thought of the mother.

Titus said, 'You're an exact copy of your mother.'

Helen chided him, 'But Titus you've taken my grandmother's picture!'

'Well yes, I — '

'You stole it!'

'I borrowed it. But then, Helen, you know I'm no saint and we have to be crafty to catch those who've stolen your worldly goods. It is vital evidence. It proves you are who you say you are. If the miniature had been left in there, it might well have been removed by anyone who didn't want us to find it.'

Helen opened her mouth to protest, but then shut it again. Titus was indeed wrong to take the little picture which was beautifully painted by the miniaturist and was set in a valuable jewelled frame, but Helen could understand the reason why he had taken it — and even applauded he had. Her grandmother wouldn't miss it because she couldn't see it anyway.

Helen whispered, 'What will your mama say when she knows you have it?'

He gave a little chuckle. 'I made sure she didn't notice when I pocketed it. I'm sure you agree she shouldn't know.'

Helen agreed then suddenly felt joyful as she realised the visit had revealed more than she had at first thought. 'Titus,' she said excitedly, 'My grandmother reminded me of my old governess, Miss Picket. I'm sure she'll be the key to unlocking many doors — I think we should search for her.

They wandered on talking about how they might locate her until some drops of rain made them take shelter in an arbour. He turned to face her and was so close for a moment or two their eyes met and then their lips began to blend in a soft kiss.

The kiss was sweet but Helen immediately drew away. Struck by the memory of Titus and Lady Sands, she shouldn't kiss a man who had her aunt as his mistress!

She attempted to control her boiling

emotions. She said stiffly, 'My aunt . . . '

'Ah,' exclaimed Titus, 'Now I think I'd better explain about her.'

'You don't have to,' Helen said quickly, moving away from him a few inches. Then she changed her mind. Unpleasant though it was, she had to know about her only other living relative. 'Yes, perhaps I ought to know about Aunt Caroline . . . and you . . . '

'I assure you I've not ravished your aunt. I thought it was necessary to place your aunt in my London house. There is no liaison between us. Not in the eyes of Society though, they thought, like you, the worst of me.'

'Oh!' she exclaimed, wanting to know more, but as the rain had ceased they came out of the shrubbery shelter into the watery sunshine and he seemed unwilling to say more on the subject, instead he asked her, 'Now tell me all you remember about Miss Picket.'

Helen said, 'Well, I can't remember much about her. I will have to think and give you more details as they occur to me. I do know, as a child, I discovered her name was Amelia and I regret to say I was very naughty and used to write it everywhere on my lesson books to tease her, which I now know was not a kind thing to do. So I fear she had no love for her over-indulged charge.'

But Titus was supportive. 'Most children have a streak of independence which makes them delight in kicking those who are in charge of them. Neither of us were perfectly behaved children, Helen.

'I shall endeavour to find Miss Picket and you shall question her and learn what you can. Also, we are to visit your old home in Mill Hill very soon which will jog your memory further.'

Overgrown and neglected, Helen's old home stood gaunt like the leafless trees around it. Still and seemingly empty.

Nevertheless a warmth crept into Helen's heart as she saw the house she had known as a child, surging back so many eventful memories.

She wiped a tear trickling down her face and smiled. No matter how dilapidated the house had become, she hoped she would soon have the money to repair it. It was her home and she was back again.

'Well. Here we are at last!' said the countess. 'I hope you've arranged for a key to be available for us, Titus.'

Helen thought the place was empty, but an old man with a bent figure appeared.

He bowed to them as they got out of the coach, but his eyes were fixed on Helen. 'Miss Martindale,' he croaked.

She smiled at him. 'And you are?'

'Bedlow, ma'am.'

The name rattled in her brain but having a slight headache from the strain of coming home didn't help Helen recollect him.

'Do you know me?' she asked peering closer at his wrinkled face.

'I recognise you, Helen. I was your father's butler.'

Helen gave a gasp. Of course, now she remembered Bedlow. The butler who she thought was an old man because she was a child. She felt joy. Here, at last, was someone who could say he knew her.

'My wife keeps the place clean, Miss Martindale, but it is covered with dust cloths. We were always hoping you'd come back one day.'

Touched by his faithfulness, Helen stepped forward and kissed the old man. 'Thank you, Bedlow.'

It was fortunate Lady Parkham and the Bedlows were chatting so much as they were being shown around the house, they didn't notice Helen's distress. And the thunderstorm, which made sudden flashes of lightning and rolling barrels of noise, made Helen feel even more sensitive about the experience. But Titus hovered nearby.

Her old nursery held a collection of old toys — and memories. 'My goodness, you must have had all the toys ever made!' exclaimed Titus.

'When I think how Charles and I used to fight to sit on our rocking horse and we had one toy castle and box of lead soldiers between us.'

'I know I had too many dolls,' sighed Helen, 'but I loved playing with them. I had no brothers or sisters to play with.'

'Indeed. You had many advantages — but you've had difficulties to overcome too.'

Feeling vulnerable Helen almost whispered, 'I don't know that I have overcome them.'

Titus smiled at her. 'You are. Keep up your spirits, Helen, as you did on that long, arduous tramp from the convent to San Sebastian. Not many ladies could have done that. And you are nearing the end of your quest now.'

Helen smiled back at him. 'Does that mean you will leave me now that you have fulfilled your obligation to return me to my home?'

Titus was torn. He knew he loved Helen and wanted her for his bride — but he didn't want to be labelled as a man who had chased after a Golden Dolly. He now had fortune of his own, but people in Society didn't know that yet. So he must wait to declare his love. Wait until the Golden Dolly jibe had faded and Society had seen Helen as she was, a beautiful young lady who was marriageable for her own sake not for her money. And no-one knew her fine character better than Titus.

Helen was distraught when he didn't deny his duty was done and he'd no plan to stay with her. She regretted he didn't care for her as much as she'd thought he did. She'd been assured she would get her property and fortune back, but alas, what she wanted most, the man she desired, seemed to be out of reach.

10

Helen suffered agonies on the way back to Parkham because painful memories kept crowding into her mind, and when the countess snoozed, she was able to talk quietly to Titus so as not to disturb his mother.

He asked softly, 'Tell me what you remember of the time just after your parents died.'

Helen knew she had to relive her terrible experience to overcome it, confront those fears she had driven into her subconscious. She knew too that she should grasp the opportunity to tell someone she could trust, someone who would understand and help her overcome the painful memories, and who better than Viscount Farringdon?

She looked into his kindly eyes, saying almost in a whisper, 'I want you to believe I'm not out for revenge, I have only the desire to come to terms with what happened to me. I want to enjoy life again as I did before those terrible things happened.'

Titus nodded, encouraging her to continue, which she did. 'I was knocked off my comfortable perch when I was told my parents had died,' she said. 'As you observed yourself today, all the luxuries in life a child could want were mine. I had good parents and was surrounded by servants. If I missed anything it was not having more relatives and friends.' Helen sighed. 'I didn't appreciate people . . . but since being in the convent I have come to see how wonderful they can be.' Helen gave a little laugh. 'I expect you thought the nuns were peculiar?'

Titus grinned. 'They saved my life.'

She nodded and continued softly, 'Yes, and they protected me too. But I was thinking of how they shared things. They taught me to be less selfish. I had no belongings of my own there. I began to value so many things in nature—'

'You were going to tell me about the time you were abducted.'

'Ah yes. In the confusion of the days that followed my parents' death, I was too young to grasp the significance of the event. The servants were at sixes and sevens because I didn't know how to tell them what they should do. A few quarrelled and I was frightened not knowing what to say to them. And some left. The cook wanted money to buy food and I had no idea how to obtain some money for it. The house was in an uproar when my Uncle and Aunt Sands came.'

The countess gave a slight snore and made Titus lean forward in his seat to ask, 'And then?'

'My uncle was, as you know, a man of grandeur. He shouted at the servants that were left and got things organised, but not of course as pleasantly for me as they used to be.'

'And your aunt?'

'Titus, you know Caroline. She's a timid creature. Afraid of my uncle. She

134

tried to be kind to me, but I didn't know her very well. Lord and Lady Sands rarely came to visit us when I was young.'

He was waiting for her to continue so Helen said, 'One thing sticks in my mind was that my uncle told the servants to pack up the valuable items in the house. All the silverware and my mother's china and jewellery were removed.

'The valuables were taken off in a carriage. Uncle Rodney told me it was for safekeeping and I was too upset to argue or overrule his decision. From being a chirpy girl, I'd become struck dumb with grief.'

'Then what happened?'

'One evening my uncle called me into my father's study and asked me if I wanted to have a holiday in a country where the sun shone, and as the days since my parent's death had seemed cold, dull and sunless, I said yes, I would like that.'

'Was your aunt there when he suggested it?'

Helen put her hands in front of her eyes. 'No,' she said thinking hard, 'I don't believe she was. We were alone at the time.'

'Ah! So where did he say you were going?'

'I can't remember. Just abroad, I think.'

Titus glanced over at his sleeping mother and asked with a low voice, 'Do you suspect Lord Sands of arranging your incarceration in the convent?'

'Heavens no! He's my uncle! A Baron of repute.'

Titus's eyebrows rose. 'So he is! How did you get to Spain then?'

'One evening, after my uncle and aunt had left my house, a strange lady and gentleman . . . well, she was a woman, not a kindly lady, and he was a man, but not a polite gentleman, came and told me to get ready to go on holiday. They said, my uncle had arranged a carriage to take me to the port.'

'That was a little odd surely?'

'I didn't think it was a trick at the time — I was excited at the thought of going on holiday.'

Helen looked out of the carriage window at the hills and trees in the distance. 'I was young and foolish,' she muttered.

'No, no, you were vulnerable. Can you recollect what those two called each other?'

Helen pursed her lips. 'No, because as soon as I was put in the carriage they had waiting, they wrapped me in a blanket to keep me warm and I could smell a strong odour and became sick, faint.'

'You'd been drugged!'

'Indeed, I must have been.'

Titus moved over to her seat and put his arm around her saying quietly, 'It was easy for them to capture and betray a young girl. Very easy. What happened next?'

Helen rested her head on his comfortable shoulder. 'I was not aware of very much. Only being lifted, carried, smothered in the blanket. Afraid at times, because I felt I couldn't breath.'

'Do you know what port you were taken to?'

'I can't.'

'And do you remember anything of the journey? What happened?'

'No, nothing. I think I was kept drugged. It made me feel ill. Mother Abbess said I was ill when I arrived at the convent, that's why they took me in.'

Titus gave a low sigh. 'Can you remember who took you to the convent?'

'Yes, there was a man. A man who took me there on a donkey. I was very sick by then.'

'And you remember nothing of this man?'

Helen was silent. She was too appalled recalling the event. Then, 'Yes!' she cried suddenly. 'I do remember now. He had a peculiar way of talking to himself, I recall. One day when I went to the stables for my morning ride on my pony I found all the grooms were gone, only this strange man seemed to be looking after the horses that remained. When alone he chatted to himself all the time. Indeed, I'm sure he was a man who took me all the way to the Pyrenees mountains.'

'He's the villain we're after,' said Titus leaning back in his seat in the carriage, 'But where do we start looking for him?'

Helen, who was making a brave recovery from her emotional day said, 'I don't suppose we'll ever hunt him down.'

Titus muttered, 'Don't give up hope. I expect someone in your parent's household will recall something about him.'

As the countess was awaking from her nap, Helen said quickly, 'Perhaps Miss Picket will remember him — if we can find her.'

'I've received a letter from Miss Picket! She says Bedlow wrote and told her I had returned,' Helen announced joyfully, coming into Lady Parkham's private parlour.

'What does she say?'

Helen beamed. 'That she is very thankful to know I'm safe and sound.'

'Anything else?'

'Well ma'am, she writes to say how happy she was working for my parents at Hendon House, which makes me believe she is not happy now. And this makes me think she seems to have gained nothing from me being forcibly removed to Spain.'

'Is Miss Picket still a governess?'

Helen frowned. 'Indeed. She writes she is teaching five children.'

'Five?' Her ladyship clasped her pearl necklace. 'Good gracious me, no wonder she thinks teaching one pupil was easier.'

Helen smiled at the good lady and then became thoughtful. Titus was in London trying to discover who was running her father's jewellery business, therefore, she couldn't wait for him to visit Miss Picket. She should go. She had the time. She was spending long hours shopping and having clothes sewn for her wardrobe suitable for her come out. But that was, for Helen, merely a diversion.

She was keen to assist with solving the puzzle of who had betrayed her. To have some information to give Titus when he returned from London. Therefore, she anticipated discovering some useful information from her old governess when a meeting was arranged.

'Yes, my dear, I think you're quite capable of managing on your own,' the countess agreed when Helen explained to her she wished to go and see Miss Picket without delay. 'You'll find our maid, Alice Morgan, a sensible woman. And our coachman is too. Unless there is a delay, or the weather turns foul, you should make the visit in one day.'

'Ma'am, I can't thank you enough.'

Lady Parkham smiled. 'Do stop thanking me. You are a delight to have around. I shall miss you when you go.'

The noise coming from the school-room was not how Helen had envisaged a lesson by Miss Picket would be conducted.

Mrs Burton, who employed Miss Picket, remarked with asperity, 'Miss Picket is not able to manage my children very well. Only she begs me to keep her on as she has no where else to go.'

Helen, who could so well have been in a similar plight had not her fortune been restored, was immediately sympathetic to her old governess. 'Maybe asking her to look after five children is too much?'

Mrs Burton bristled. 'They are all well behaved — if she would only use the whip. She's too soft with them.'

Helen recalled Miss Picket had never used a whip on her, although the nuns did and it did nothing to cure her misbehaviour.

When the schoolroom door was swung open the chaos was obvious. A painting lesson was in progress, but no painting was taking place.

Only one child was seated in a desk. The others were playing about. Two boys were hanging out of the window admiring the Parkham coach in the drive below.

Helen felt a surge of emotion seeing her old governess again. It took a moment or two for her to control her desire to rush up and hug her.

Miss Picket, a skinny lady, her hair straggling from her cap and over her rather prominent nose on which perched her spectacles, was wearing a gown so old Helen was sure she recognised it.

She was bending over a child giving instruction on how the paint should be applied, while another boy was dancing about and making faces behind her back. The smallest child, who was about four years old, was munching an apple from the bowl of apples set out for the children to paint.

'Children, children!' shouted Mrs Burton, clapping her hands. 'There will be no honey for your tea for this disgraceful behaviour.'

Helen had difficulty not to laugh as the children, caught red-handed at their naughtiness, slide back into their schoolroom desks and taking up their paint brushes began to work as if they had been sitting there studying quietly all afternoon.

But Helen's smile was swept away when she saw the expression of defeat on Miss Picket's face. 'Mrs Burton, I, er, we were having a painting session which is always a little . . . ' Poor Miss Picket was lost for words.

'Dear Miss Picket,' Helen said, rushing towards the worn-out lady and taking her hands, as red-faced Miss Picket tried to curtsey. 'How delighted I am to see you again.'

'Miss Martindale!' Miss Picket cried, her eyes flashing joy behind her spectacles, 'You're looking so well — I am pleased.'

Helen turned to Mrs Burton. 'May I have the opportunity to talk to my old governess, ma'am? We have so much to discuss.'

Mrs Burton's large bosom heaved. 'Well, I don't know. Who is to look after the children?'

Helen was tempted to say they were her children and she could look after them herself. But she smiled. 'Perhaps a little extra playtime would not come amiss?'

Mrs Burton raised her voice, 'I do not approve of play, Miss Martindale. As well Miss Picket knows. Miss Picket is a disaster as a schoolteacher. I should dismiss her.'

The children lifted their heads from their work and smirked at each other. Those remarks said in front of the children, considered Helen, were insufferable. Miss Picket's self esteem was being crushed. She obviously couldn't cope with the rowdy youngsters. Children needed discipline, but also time to play and use their imagination and energy. Preventing them from playing was senseless. Criticising their teacher in front of the children was unhelpful — to say the least.

Helen was determined from that moment to take Miss Picket from her unsatisfactory position. Not releasing Miss Picket's hand she said, in a firm voice, not unlike the mother abbess's at the convent, 'Seeing as you are not wanted here, Miss Picket, you shall come home with me.'

Helen turned to address amazed Mrs Burton. 'Miss Picket may be unsatisfactory for you, ma'am, but she is just who I want as a companion. You can send your older children to school, ma'am. There are schools aplenty which employ the cane to keep children under order.'

Mrs Burton gaped like a fish as Helen continued, 'Miss Picket put up with my waywardness when I was a child and now she needs to retire from the hurly burly of the classroom.'

Mrs Burton huffed. If it were not for the fact that Miss Martindale behaved like an exceedingly rich young lady and had arrived in Lord Parkham's very fine coach, with a formidable looking older maid, who would support Miss Martindale, she should try contradicting her or challenging her visitor's decision to take the governess away.

11

After Miss Picket was installed at Parkham House as Miss Martindale's companion, the Countess of Parkham was content to retire from the constant attention she'd been giving Helen for the past few months. The Countess told the Earl of Parkham, as they retired one evening, 'Miss Amelia Picket is a most agreeable lady. She and Helen have become good friends.'

'Humph!' exclaimed the Earl. 'I'd like to know when young Titus is going to marry Miss Martindale, and move into Parkham Court, so we can go to the Dower House, which is all the space we need nowadays. This barn of a place is draughty.'

'You are jumping the gun, dear,' declared his countess. 'Titus is still hunting down the people who stole from the gel. And she won't be ready to think of marriage until it is all settled.'

'What if Titus is not able to nail the villains?'

His wife smiled confidently. 'You really should have more confidence in your younger son, dear. Titus has been tracking down the enemy for years. And very successful he was too. Why else did the Duke of Wellington award him a special medal?'

'Because he said himself, he was lucky.'

Lady Parkham smiled in agreement. 'Indeed, Titus has been fortunate in many ways. But he did climb out of the mire by himself, and I agree Helen Martindale will make him a splendid wife — if she is willing.'

The earl grunted. 'She won't if he don't ask her to marry him. If he's still chasing around the country after a fox or two that won't be caught. He can't give me a grandson!'

Lady Parkham gave a merry laugh. 'Well, dear, we shall see. I think Titus is still busy trying to discover what happened to little Helen Martindale years ago, and she needs a little more time to come to terms with her changed life. I don't think Hendon House will ever be her home again. It holds too many memories for her.'

Titus couldn't wait to see Helen again. She'd become a charming lady in her fine new clothes and easy manners, and he realised he was not the only gentleman to be interested in her company. His mother was making sure her young guest was enjoying a social life in London, meeting others of her age and attending functions where she could dance — which Helen loved.

Helen thought he was avoiding her because he was frequently absent when his mother thought he should be escorting her to functions. But, in fact, he was occupied seeking the criminals who had abducted her.

He'd avoided telling Society he'd inherited his brother's position and title, so that to many he was still Mr Stonely, the almost penniless younger son of an earl, who'd been disinherited. Many considered him an officer on half pay. And others thought him disgraceful because he kept Lady Sands as his mistress in his London house.

With this low reputation he could slide into his old London gambling haunts and hear the gossip. Gradually he was putting together the information he needed.

To the Bow Street runners it really didn't matter whether he was plain Mr Stonely or Viscount Farringdon. They were as anxious as he was to find the perpetrators of crimes.

'We've found Bill Scroggs,' one Bow Street runner had informed him when they met him in London.

'Good!' declared Titus. He was the man Miss Picket had told him had worked in the stables after Helen's parents had died — and he'd talked to himself all the time.

'Not so good,' rejoined the runner. 'He had a knife in his throat.'

Titus put his hand to his own throat.

'The crime gets deeper,' he commented with a shiver. 'Bill Scroggs could have murdered Miss Martindale. But he did not. It makes me think some other evil mind was behind her kidnap. And now they know we are on his trail they've got rid of Scroggs to hide the truth.'

'We agree, my lord. Bill Scroggs showed no signs of having made a profit from his part in the abduction. So we agree he could not bring himself to murder the girl, so he took her to a remote convent in Spain instead. And the real villain, finding Miss Martindale has come back to England hale and hearty, was keen to silence the fellow.'

'So who in the end gained by the girl being missing?'

All three men said in unison, 'Lord Rodney Sands.'

However, how were they going to prove Lord Sands was guilty of treating his wife cruelly? Of stealing from his niece, and having her abducted? And now, it seemed he'd arranged to have killed the man who drugged Helen and carted her to Spain.

Helen regretted she had no jewellery to wear with her new clothes. As she was known as the heiress of a well-known London jeweller, it puzzled fashionable ladies too. Helen could, of course, have bought some. But she was on the lookout for the jewellery her mother wore. They were not just valuable, well-designed jewellery that her father had given her mother, they were pieces with sentimental value for her.

One glittering social evening she recognised her mother's emerald necklace around the neck of a young lady. She stood wondering what she should do when she became aware of someone approaching her.

Her heart plummeted as she saw the stout figure of her Uncle Rodney glaring at her.

'Oh dear!' she said, looking wildly for an escape. Titus was supposed to be with her that evening — but he was late coming, as usual.

Uncle Rodney's waddle was all the more noticeable compared with the dancers smooth steps to the music. His short height was obvious to her as it hadn't been when she was small herself. But there was the florid, wide face and small eyes, and the plump, moist lips she remembered. She gave him a polite curtsy.

His bow was slight. 'Well, niece. So you are back.'

Helen tried to smile pleasantly.

He was clearly taken aback that his niece could be so composed. The frightened little girl he had dealt with all those years ago had gone. He recognised a mature lady faced him now, and he was not able to quell her easily.

Helen decided she didn't like him any more than she did as a girl. But she would not drag up the past. What was the point in asking him why he had promised her a holiday, and then found it was a trick to abduct her abroad? He might not have had anything to do with what happened to her. When it happened, he was abroad. But he could have answered her letters sent from the convent. So why had he not?

She could ask him about her mother's jewels, and many other questions she would have liked the answer to but she found she couldn't. In fact, she decided she would endeavour to have as little to do with him in the future as possible.

Rodney Sands took a pinch of snuff and then sneezed before saying, 'I don't think your damaged reputation will recover.'

Helen's back straightened. 'My reputation has not been damaged.'

She didn't like his smile. It was false. Untrustworthy. Neither did she like his insinuation that her reputation had been ruined. But she refused to show how hurtful his remark was. Perhaps he felt he wanted to kick back at her after she had taken back her money from him?

'Anyway you'll find it difficult to

marry now,' he went on, 'perhaps you should go back to the convent?'

Gasping for breath, Helen looked down at her slippers, and waved her fan in front of her blazing cheeks. Trying not to burst out in fury at his insensitive remark, she replied calmly, 'No, I shall not return to the convent. I shall marry, uncle. In fact, I've already decided who is to be my husband.'

He didn't seem to like her quick response to say she intended to marry. She saw his nostrils flare. And she knew why, her marriage would definitely put him out of line for inheriting anything from her.

She felt uncomfortable and didn't feel she could question him. And he had nothing more to say to her and abruptly bowed and walked off.

Helen was quite sure now that she not only disliked her uncle, but she began to wonder if he was trustworthy. She decided to do an investigation of her own.

Her thoughts and eyes went to the

young lady who was wearing her mother's jewellery, and when she got the chance, near the end of the evening, she slipped over to talk to her.

The bright green precious stones had attracted Helen when she was a child, and her mama had told her that she would have them when she grew up. And so Helen could recognise the setting, and as few jewels were as fine as those from Martindales, it was unlikely there could be another necklace made like it.

'Your necklace is lovely,' Helen commented as she came close enough to examine the necklace again.

The lady smiled at the compliment. 'Thank you, ma'am. My husband acquired it for my birthday a month ago.'

As Helen continued to admire it that lady went on, 'I must admit I would not have chosen it.'

Helen bent her head forward as she looked more closely at the jewels. 'Oh, why is that?'

'They are too green for me to wear with many of my gowns. I would prefer pearls.'

Helen thought quickly. 'Indeed? And I should love some emeralds. Do you think you could ask him where he got them from?'

The lady tapped her fan on her lanky husband's arm. The scholarly looking man, with a receding chin, looked alarmed when his wife asked him, 'William, this young lady would like to know where you acquired my emerald necklace.'

He stuttered uneasily, 'I hope, I pray, she is not saying they were stolen?'

'No, no,' Helen assured him. 'It is just that I love emeralds and hoped you could tell me where you bought them.'

'Ah. Now I have to admit I acquired them second-hand from Covent Garden.'

He was embarrassed and Helen knew why. Covent Garden sold fruit and vegetables, but the neighbourhood surrounding the popular theatres in Drury Lane and Bow Street, had acquired a dubious reputation.

Helen wanted to dispel any guilt on his part, so she gave him an encouraging grin, 'I expect you won them as a gambling debt?'

'Actually, I did.'

'And which gambling den did you acquire them?'

'Prance's, was the name. I was offered the jewels and liked them, but my wife ain't so keen on 'em.'

'Well, I love them,' Helen assured the couple. She hesitated to ask about the gambling den, it seemed too inquisitive. Not something a young lady should probe into.

The gentleman said, 'I was told and I believe it is true that these jewels came originally from Martindales. The best jewellers in London.'

'I thought they were. You see, I am Helen Martindale.'

The eyes that stared back at her made Helen wonder what they might say. But the lady gave her a sweet smile. 'We heard your story, Miss Martindale, and were so glad you escaped. It is wonderful to see you here, looking well.'

Helen breathed more easily. 'Thank you. You may wonder why I ask about your jewels. Actually, I should tell you, they belonged to my mother. That is why I am keen to know about them.'

'Then you shall have them back,' cried the lady.

'Indeed you shall,' agreed her husband.

Helen was touched by their insistence that she should have her mother's necklace back. She said quickly, 'I suggest we make an exchange. I'll accept the emeralds, and make sure you have a Martindale pearl necklace to replace it. One you can select from the shop, ma'am.'

The young lady was overjoyed by the suggestion. As they were discussing the jewels, and exchanging names and addresses, Lord Farringdon appeared to claim Helen for the waltz.

When they were dancing, Helen was

able to tell Titus what she had just discovered. He knew where Prance's establishment was, and told her he would plan to make enquires there. Perhaps more of Helen's jewellery would be found.

'I'll accompany you,' Helen said, 'because I might be able to recognise some pieces.'

'It's not the kind of establishment ladies visit,' he warned.

Helen gave him a smile. 'I've been to many places most ladies would not visit.'

He smiled back. 'So you have. Then, I'd be glad of your assistance.'

12

Titus hoped the gun hidden under his coat would not show. He also hoped the Bow Street Runners were on hand too as he escorted Helen into the coffee shop.

Prance was known by the Bow Street Runners for running a gaming hall, but he was also suspected of other crimes. Selling valuables gained from bets was one lucrative business he was engaged in. Any cove who offered him a gold watch or a silver candlestick, instead of money to bet on and then lost it to the bank, Prance would sell.

Titus had found out that the coffee house in Covent Garden was frequented by Prance and it was where he sold those valuable items for what he could get for them.

Sometimes when a valuable piece of jewellery, like a Martindale piece came his way, Prance would not find it difficult to persuade an honest young man to buy it for his wife, or ladybird, just as the emerald necklace he had recently sold. But as his gambling clients were often engaged in shady dealings, Prance knew he had to be careful.

Helen, seated at the coffee shop table in Covent Garden, was told to keep her eyes open. 'What for?' Helen asked Titus.

'Because I want to see if you recognise someone who is coming in shortly. No, don't look round yet. I don't want the person to see you first or they may slip away.'

A short time later Titus noticed a man who'd just come in. He was alone and dressed in a dark coat and breeches. With quick strides he paced through the aisles of tables. He appeared to be looking for someone.

Once Helen's eyes were on the odd-looking character he seemed to fascinate her. She continued to watch him as he stopped by one customer, drew something from his coat pocket, and showed it to the seated man. After the man had shaken his head, the object was pushed back into his pocket. Helen guessed he was trying to sell something.

It was when the dark man reached their aisle and began approaching their table that the man's face, which had been hidden under his hat, became visible.

A little cry escaped Helen's lips because she recognised the screwed-up features and the narrowed crafty eyes and she trembled. She shook so much grasping the table that the coffee cups rattled. She stuttered, 'Titus . . . that man . . . I'm sure he took me when I was a child. Oh!' Overcome by the sudden awful memory of the stressful event, her years at the convent had almost obliterated, Helen crumpled into a faint.

Titus was caught between assisting Helen from sliding on to the floor and catching the man she had accused.

Prance saw both Helen swoon and Titus's dilemma. He was lightening quick. With a sleight of hand he produced a knife and threw it with expert skill at Titus.

The knife blade thudded into the wooden beam just above Titus's head because Titus had bent down a second before to tend to Helen. Prance leapt away to remove himself from the coffee house. And he would have done so successfully, except that in front of him stood a Bow Street Runner holding a pistol which was pointed at him.

Prance turned to make for the back of the shop only to find another Bow Street Runner blocking his way.

But he was fast, was Prance, nimble on his feet, and able to jump over a table like an acrobat and avoid his pursuers. Upsetting the customers who yelled and tried to catch him, he'd just made the door when a single bullet stung him on the leg and felled him.

'I say, crack shot, sir!' cried a startled

customer looking over to where Viscount Farringdon, late of the 95th rifles, held his smoking gun.

As the Bow Street Runners pounced on Prance and led him away the confusion in the coffee shop subsided as people came over to where Titus now sat on the floor with Helen resting in his arms.

'Is the young lady all right, sir?'

'Indeed, she's not been injured. Just frightened. I'll call my coachman and take her home. No, it will be quicker to take her to my London house where her aunt, Lady Sands can administer to her.'

The carriage stopped in front of a small, but elegant Georgian House. 'This is where I live,' announced Titus getting out of the carriage, 'and this is where we'll get the best coffee in London.'

He helped Helen out on to the pavement. 'Welcome to my home, Helen,' he said, taking her hand.

Helen looked up and admired the

proportions of the house, the fine stonework and black railings and ironwork canopy over the shiny front door. Titus walked up the steps and opened the front door bowing to allow her to enter before him.

'Titus!' cried a delighted child's voice and a pretty little girl came bounding down the staircase into his arms. The viscount swung her up so that she could put her arms around his neck with much laughter from both child and man.

'This young lady is Sophie,' he said informally.

The older lady coming down the stairs after the child stood on the steps and tutted. 'I'm sorry, Titus,' she said, 'Sophie should learn not to throw herself into your arms the moment you come home. Especially when you are bringing a guest.'

Helen stood mesmerised. The lady's voice sounded just like her mother's. In fact the lady looked just like she remembered her mother. A surge of joy overcame her making tears come to her eyes.

'Helen, this is your Aunt Caroline,' said Titus.

'And I'm Sophie Sands,' shrilled the little girl.

Helen looked at Titus quite puzzled until her aunt kissed her and explained, 'Yes indeed. I had a baby to protect when Titus kindly took me in. That's why he gave me the use of his London house and took a commission.'

Helen wasn't surprised Lady Sands had left her husband, when she knew how nasty her Uncle Rodney was, but she was too bemused to comment, so when the visitors were escorted into the parlour and Aunt Caroline and her daughter went to get some refreshment, Titus explained, 'Your cousin, Sophie, is a lively child and gives her mother much pleasure. And I'm glad of it. When I was away at the war the little one was able to occupy Caroline's time, but now Sophie is seven years of age and is ready for schooling, Both mother and child need fresh companions.'

Helen was delighted to have met two charming relatives. Aunt Caroline was clearly grateful to Titus for giving her and her child refuge when she was in dire need. It explained why her aunt was living in Titus's home and that there was no romantic affair between her aunt and Titus.

Also it confirmed Helen's suspicion that her Uncle Rodney was a rogue, and days later, it was reinforced, when Titus informed her that Prance had informed the magistrate that her uncle had been the instigator of her abduction years ago and had told Prance to kill Scroggs.

'It is sad,' Titus told Helen as he took her for a drive through Hyde Park in his curricle on a bright summer morning, 'your Uncle Rodney had no need of your fortune, for he was well breeched. He was just greedy and saw the opportunity to dispose of you as a child.'

'What will happen to him?'

'Sir Rodney Sands and Prance will hang for the murder of Bill Scroggs. They are also guilty of other crimes as you know.'

Helen bowed her head. After a few minutes silence she enquired, 'And what will happen to Aunt Caroline? Can she ever get over the harm done to her?'

Titus turned and smiled at her. 'You should know the answer to that, my dear.'

Helen remained thoughtful. After a while she said, 'Yes, I believe it is possible to get over the tragedy. Society might look askance at us for a while, not because we have done anything wrong, but because we have been harmed by the wickedness of others near to us. But we'll recover.'

Titus flicked the reins and the horses quickened their pace, striding out and drawing the carriage through the park. As Titus removed his hat to greet other carriage passengers passing by, he asked, 'Do you like your Aunt Caroline?'

'Indeed I do. She reminds me of mama. I'll be visiting her.'

'She has need of good friends now that she will be moving back into the Sands house. Many in Society may shun her. Although I believe she is no longer a frightened young wife and has gained self esteem.'

'Thanks to you, Titus.'

'I like to think I've done some good amongst all the bad things in my past.'

Helen said quickly, 'You've done a lot for me too.' She waited for his response but was disappointed he didn't say he had a high regard for her. He just turned and gave her the warmest smile.

The musical evening was held at a socialite's grand London house. Being near the end of the season, Helen was now used to social occasions and meeting people. She had made friends, just as if she had never been subjected to eight years incarcerated in a Spanish convent.

But she was unmarried. Uninterested in offers of marriage. Only one man she craved for, and he was showing little interest in her. Other hopeful brides milled around him. He had a plentiful choice of pretty young ladies to choose from.

Only she knew Titus well, his faults and failings as well as his fine qualities. She also knew he required more than a pretty miss to satisfy his adventurous spirit, someone who understood him. She wondered if he thought she didn't care for him, and she had to find out and show him she loved him.

It was one of those balmy summer evenings and Helen felt restless after the refreshment break. It was quite tiring for her trying to appear composed and enjoying the singing, when her heart was playing a different tune.

She needed to keep an eye on Viscount Farringdon without appearing to do so, which made her wish she was a fly with eyes on the back of her head. Not that he could move once the concert had started. She could spy him reflected in a huge mirror at the side of the room. And he appeared as restless as she did.

They had greeted each other cordially enough as they met at the start of the concert. But, as she had planned, she had pretended not to be other than frostily polite to him. Normally on meeting they would exchange a few words and enjoy a quiet chuckle about something, but this evening Helen had deliberately avoided any pleasantries. She wanted him to feel ignored. As if she really didn't mind if he was there or not.

He was shuffling his feet. Made his father glare at him once or twice for fidgeting and he seemed to spend more time studying his long-fingered hands and his programme than admiring the contralto.

When refreshment time came, Helen quickly accepted the invitation of a suitor she had known for some time to accompany her to the refreshment room and noticed as she stood sipping her lemonade, that Titus was alone and pacing the floor like a caged lion.

So far so good. Titus, Viscount Farringdon, looked decidedly uneasy but was it because of her or for some other reason? Helen had to know.

When the concert resumed she congratulated herself that she had hardly glanced at him directly the whole evening. She had observed him via the mirror, but was she playing with fire? Could she have overdone ignoring him?

Sick with fright that she was making a mistake, Helen became quite overcome with panic.

She had to get out of the crowded, hot atmosphere of the room and into the cool night air.

Excusing herself to Lady Parkham, in between one of the songs, she left the recital hall and walked out into the garden for some fresh air. It was indecorous to leave without a chaperon, but Helen felt she could hardly breathe if she stayed inside any longer. And being a private home, there was less stigma for her to leave on her own than there would have been if the concert were being held in a public concert hall.

Free at last from the stuffy hall and from leading Titus a dance, Helen strolled around the garden.

In front of her was a delightful garden pond. In the middle of the pond, a carved stone fish fountain spouted water that splashed in a spray that prettily caught the garden lights.

It was so pleasant to sit on the edge of the pond and to hear in the distance the fine singer while watching the water display.

Helen felt better. The air was delightful, filled with scented roses from a bush nearby.

She didn't attempt to think about anything. She was only aware that she was living in a little paradise for a while.

Then she fancied paddling in the cool water. As a nun she was used to being barefoot, and on warm days it was a good feeling to be free of the constriction of shoes. Rebellious, and not caring what others might think should she be seen, as her reputation was already questionable, she decided she not only longed to dip her feet in the water, but she would do it.

So Helen slipped off her shoes and stockings, bunched up her dress and slid into the water.

Although some of the fish were a little startled, it seemed perfectly natural for her to be moving gently in the water. Calf-deep the water ran deliciously through her toes, while a little of the spray from the fountain touched her hair, her face and arms.

She gave a little laugh but then she frowned. Someone was crunching along the garden path towards the fountain.

She couldn't hide. She couldn't get out of the water fast enough. She was stuck and a little angry to find her pleasure interrupted.

But, thankfully she saw who it was.

'Gracious!' she declared, 'I'm glad it's only you, Titus. You gave me a fright.'

He stood with his feet apart, his hands linked behind his head and laughed.

'What's so funny?'

'You are amusing me. Young ladies do not behave like you — but then you are not a typical young lady.'

'No,' agreed Helen a little sadly, 'but you know what I have suffered.'

'Indeed, you've had much to overcome and I admire you and I think you're sensible to be cooling yourself on this hot evening. May I join you?'

Helen chuckled. 'I don't know if there is room enough for us both, it's only a small fountain.'

'We'll snuggle up,' he said sitting on the edge of the pond and quickly removing his silver-buckled shoes and socks, and rolling up his pantaloon legs.

Plop. He almost jumped into the water and splashed his feet about joyfully.

'Steady on, Titus. I don't want to be soaked.'

'I wasn't thinking of drowning you.'

'Then why are you holding me?'

'So you don't get away.'

Helen looked up at his smiling face. 'I don't intend to. It's nice in the water, isn't it?'

He bent to kiss her and she didn't back away. Somehow it seemed right for them to want to hold each other close, to touch lips.

What people would think who happened to see them did not occur to either of them. As the concert ended and people drifted off, one carriage was left behind. It belonged to Viscount Farringdon and his parents had been informed that their son would bring Miss Martindale home so they had left too.

Only the two in the pond remained. They had so much to talk about, plans to make. The amused hostess sent her butler out in the garden with two glasses of champagne, as she was sure it would be welcome. And it was.

'My dear water nymph,' said Titus, 'will you do me the honour to be my bride?'

178

Helen smiled with happiness, her feet sending her on a little dance through the water.

He seemed a little concerned she did not answer at once, so he added, 'I promise my old ways, like my old name and reputation as Captain Stonely, are gone forever. I will be true to you, Helen.'

'And I too will be glad to rid myself of my name, Helen Martindale, the abducted heiress and Golden Dolly, and become your viscountess.'

'And so it shall be.'

Holding their champagne glasses they drank and kissed again.

The butler, who had seen some strange things during his time in service but nothing as strange as this couple embracing under the fountain, hurried into the house to fetch a couple of drying towels.

AT SEAGULL BAY

Catriona McCuaig

When Florence Williams and her sister Edie inherit houses at Seagull Bay they decide to set themselves up as seaside landladies, catering to summer visitors. There, Florence's daughters become mixed up with two wildly unsuitable young men. Flattered by the attentions of an unscrupulous entertainer, Vicky tries to elope, but is brought back in time. Having learned that holiday romances seldom last, her prim sister, Alice, wonders if true love will ever come her way.

A TIME TO RUN

Janet Whitehead

When nurse Lynn Crane finds employment at an isolated manor house in the Yorkshire countryside, all is not what it seems. As she nurses her attractive patient, Serge Varda, Prince of Estavia, an alarming truth emerges: her employers, Max Ozerov and the sinister Dr Miros, his countrymen, plan to wrest control of the country from him. The young couple escape from almost certain death, but, as Serge is eventually restored to state duties, will he share them with Lynne?

PRESCRIPTION FOR HAPPINESS

Patricia Posner

From their very first meeting, sparks fly between Rose and Matthew. But they soon discover they have a lot in common — both are coping with loss, and both have a parentless child to love and care for. Their young nieces become best friends, and want nothing more than for all of them to become a family. But even though Rose and Matthew help each other through tough times, neither of them are sure they can get over their past hurts to love again . . .

GHOST WRITER

Catriona McCuaig

When Fiona Flint loses her job as a reporter at the Marston Chronicle she becomes a ghost writer, helping senior citizens to publish their memoirs. While interviewing one of her clients, Jason Greaves, she meets his great nephew, Aaron Parker, whom she suspects of trying to defraud elderly investors. Fiona persuades Jeremy Dean, a former colleague, to help her investigate. Jeremy hopes to rekindle their romance, but can she ever forgive the mistake he made in the past?

DANCE WITH ME

Janet Chamberlain

Line dance instructor Lisa Gates desperately needs a new venue, and has her heart set on the Cliff Hotel. The new owner, shrewd business-man Ken Huntley, has plans to revamp the building, and is adamant Lisa's classes won't fit its elite new image. However, in an amazing about turn, he agrees to accommo-date her for a brief period preceding the refurbishment — on the proviso that he works alongside her as her DJ. What can she do but agree . . . ?

WHERE THE SUN SHINES BRIGHTER

Jennifer Bohnet

Nicola, a young mother, is black-mailed into moving to France with Oliver, her son, for the sake of his inheritance. Full of reservations as she leaves behind her long-term friend Andrew, she must also face Henri, her interfering ex-father-in-law. Nicola finds getting to know her French relatives and making a life for herself and Oliver a challenge. And, attracted to Gilles Bongars, working nearby, how will she react to Andrew's plan to start a new life in France with her?